D1435984

A Grizzly Revenged

Mayle Stone, a young fur trapper, lives with Izusa, a Cherokee woman whom he received as 'payment' for a wolfskin from a Cherokee brave. During a visit to Fort St Vrain for supplies, Izusa comes to the attention of an outlaw, Jon Rudyman, who plans to kill the trapper and take the woman. The plan has flaws, however, and Stone survives, but Izusa disappears.

Hence, Stone is out for revenge. But also looking for Rudyman is bounty hunter Rey Heston. It's a race to see who will track down Rudyman first.

By the same author

Robbery in Savage Pass
Kato's Army
The Comanche's Revenge
The Comanche Fights Again
Incident at Fall Creek

A Grizzly Revenged

D.M. Harrison

A Black Horse Western

ROBERT HALE

ISBN 978-0-7198-2505-7

The Crowood Press
The Stable Block
Crowood Lane
Ramsbury
Marlborough
Wiltshire SN8 2HR

www.bhwesterns.com

Robert Hale is an imprint
of The Crowood Press

Typeset by
Derek Doyle & Associates, Shaw Heath
Printed and bound in Great Britain by
CPI Group (UK) Ltd, Croydon, CR0 4YY

CHAPTER ONE

A young boy stood in the doorway and watched as his pa took his gun and placed it in his mouth. No mean feat as the longrifle wasn't a gun to play with – yet here was a man determined to say goodbye to life. On the table stood a quarter of a bottle of rot-gut whiskey, the rest, the boy assumed, was in his father.

'Don't do it, Pa,' he said.

Kirk Stone, paused, lowered the gun and stared in his direction.

'Sorry, son. My dreams are all about tuckered out.' He looked at the piece of rock next to the whiskey bottle. For a brief moment it sparkled as an indifferent shaft of sunlight lit it up. Then it turned to a grey rock again.

His son pointed to the rock. 'You've made it, Pa. You've found gold.'

Kirk Stone laughed. 'You know what this is?' The question was rhetorical; he didn't wait for an answer. 'It's Pyrite. Or Fool's Gold. I found me this piece and went to get it weighed. You know what, Mayle? They damn near laughed me out of the Assay Office.'

Those were his final words.

*

Much later, after his ma's hysterics, after the lawman had visited to make sure there'd been no foul play and promised to say it was an accident, and after Pa's friends took the body to the carpenter, who made plenty of money from coffins and burials, it was time for Mayle Stone to get a bucket and a rag. Slowly, he cleared up the blood and the fragments of brains from the walls and floor. Every time he paused to rinse and wring the cloth, he cursed his pa for not having the good manners to go into the woods or mountains and save his son a whole heap of work.

Ma tried to explain Pa's demise to her nippers. 'He found living out West too hard.'

'Ain't taking your own life a sin, Ma?'

'You were always too sharp for your own good, Mayle,' Ma said, as she cuffed his ear. 'We all got to say it was an accident, remember?'

Twelve lots of heads nodded in unison. 'Of course, he'll have to explain the reason to the man in the sky.'

She smiled but Mayle knew she was angry because before the other nippers found out, she'd cursed loudly, to him as well as his pa.

'I hope he gets sent straight to the devil for leaving me alone with all these mouths to feed.'

Mayle Stone rushed home to tell Ma the news as soon as possible. As he retraced his steps, he reflected on his life – he'd lived at Pike's Peak for quite a few years. The dream his pa had believed would make them millionaires hadn't materialized. However, Mayle's friends from the Cherokee camp had told him about a new gold strike near the South Platte River. He was privy to this information because his great great grandmother on his mother's side had been a Cherokee.

He didn't find Ma but the new pa, Bert Turner, who sat

in the chair nearest the fire, greeted Mayle's news with scorn.

'Tol' you to keep away from those Injuns,' he said. Mayle knew well enough not to mention that Ma was one-eighth Cherokee and had a good dollop of their blood, because that kind of remark didn't go down well. 'I'll find the gold here. It's just sitting waiting for me. Just 'cause your ol' pa was a loser, don't mean I can't succeed.'

Mayle mumbled, bit at his lip and then looked down at the floor. Pa Turner's face went puce.

'What did you say?'

'I didn't say anything,' Mayle said. However, he couldn't resist adding, 'I thought you're too lazy to do anything but I didn't say it.'

Bert moved out of the chair with a speed not consistent with such a large man. Mayle moved fast, but not fast enough.

Mayle Stone left home soon after that.

Looking back, he couldn't blame Pa Turner entirely because Stone knew his resentment showed through in everything he said and did. He told Ma she'd found someone before his pa's chair was cold. That comment and his unfriendliness to Turner had made it too difficult to stay with his family. He knew, realistically, in the western settlements where women were scarce, it had been unlikely that his ma would be single for long.

In retrospect, the new pa was OK but at almost fourteen years, Mayle reckoned he was old enough to leave – and that two men vying for status in a household was like two women in a kitchen: one was bound to get upset. The final push to branch out on his own was when Pa Turner said, 'If you get to thinking you got some power in this house, try ordering my dog around. He knows who is master.'

The pit bull terrier snarled, drool pooled around its

7

mouth and dripped on to the floor.

'Yeah, you're the master here, Pa Turner,' Stone agreed.

When he left, he took the only thing his pa had left behind – the longrifle. The gun that had deprived his pa of a head was in a box under Ma's bed so Stone helped himself. No one wanted it. Light in weight, the longrifle had many attributes; it was graceful – and as his pa had demonstrated – fatally precise. Stone reckoned he'd aim it the other way and not risk the same 'accident' that had occurred to Kirk Stone.

He took no victuals. There was no surplus food, ever, in their home. He aimed to survive off the land. He'd worked out that squirrels and rabbits were easy enough to trap. The bigger game would wait until he'd found a place to stay for more than a few days. And the surplus skins he could trade for ammunition – shot and gunpowder.

'Ain't you 'fraid of the Injuns?'

His younger brother, ten-year-old Levee, had watched his preparations to leave.

'Nah! Don't forget we all got a bit of Cherokee blood. You remember those times we hunted with White Pony and Fast Runner? They showed us sign language. That'll help persuade those Injuns not to scalp me!'

'You ain't big enough to leave us,' Levee complained. 'Pa used to say you're so thin you could take a bath in a shotgun barrel.'

He started to laugh as he rubbed Levee's head and tousled his hair. Levee pulled away. 'I ain't a child,' he grumbled.

'That's true. You'll soon be full grown.' He knelt down to be eye to eye to him. 'Don't worry about me, little 'un.' The laughter sounded hollow as he added, 'Keep outta Pa Turner's way and leave home as soon as you can.'

*

The weather was kind to him and allowed him to travel fast. He didn't have to hole up for weeks and slow his journey down – within months he was halfway up the trail to the South Platte River.

However, the unseasonably warm weather brought a problem he hadn't expected. Too late he recalled his old pa's words. 'Warm temperatures disturb an animal's hibernation but a warm winter spell doesn't guarantee food will be available for the hungry creatures.'

He felt goose bumps on his neck. He wasn't cold – it was the sound of the growling animal that had alerted him to danger. His normal defence for bear encounters was to avoid them. At any time of year, a bear could be an ornery creature but to find one awake when it should be asleep was bad news.

Stone could see the creature, which was far too near to him, as it stood upright at about seven foot six inches. He guessed its weight at 600 pounds. It was a young male or a female bear – he couldn't tell – but whatever it was, it looked decidedly grumpy. Stone guessed it to be a grizzly. It had a pronounced shoulder hump and very large claws.

His first instinct was to back away, slowly, keeping an eye on it and be ready for anything the bear might do. He scanned the vista for a tree high enough to scale but the only ones he saw would be ideal for the grizzly to chase after him. Unless of course he could make it up at least sixty feet up the tree and get there much faster than the bear.

Memories of his pa's advice popped into his head. 'Fall to cover the belly, protect yer head and neck with yer hands and then spread the elbows and legs so the grizzly can't flip yer over. An' lie perfectly still.'

9

'And then what'll happen?'

'Might chew you up a bit, but it'll get tired and go away if it don't think you're a threat.'

'And what if it likes the taste of you and keeps chawin', Pa?'

His answer had been, 'Then get up and fight. Either way, you're a goner. I think it's better to go out fighting.'

Wryly, Stone wished his pa had followed his own advice a year ago. Then perhaps now he wouldn't be facing a grizzly. He didn't like the idea of being snacked on but now, as he looked at the grizzly, he knew running away to be the lesser evil. He didn't want to get chewed and spat out.

Stone's gaze followed the creature as he edged back. It was then he felt fear. According to his pa, fear didn't kick in until later and then he'd air his paunch and suffer the trots for days afterwards!

However, he wasn't afraid for himself. The grizzly hadn't noticed him – he was eyeing up something else. A woman. A Cherokee Indian woman.

Stone took his longrifle, always prepped and ready to fire, and started to move towards the bear. He shouted at the woman, 'Get down. Lie on the ground.' He signed and hoped she'd understand because he couldn't do anymore to help.

At the new sounds the bear dropped to all fours. It popped its jaws, swatted the ground with its front paws and blew and snorted air from its nostrils. Stone couldn't recall whether this meant it was about to attack or if it was bluffing.

'Let's not have a fight, Mr Grizzly.' He stared it straight in the eyes to let it know he wasn't fooling. He stamped his feet. 'I don't want to hurt you.'

Stone hoped the look on his face said 'I'm gonna kill

10

you' and not 'go away, please'. It was then the grizzly decided to attack. Unfortunately the bear seemed to have guessed at the latter, not the former interpretation of Stone's facial movements and again it stood up and the forest echoed with an almighty roar.

Although Mayle Stone was a good height for a youth, he felt the shadow of the grizzly blot out the daylight as it towered above him.

Stone continued to shout. He had no intention of allowing the bear to win without a fight.

'Aim for the face – mouth, eyes and nose,' a voice in Stone's head encouraged him. At that moment, all Stone could see was the grizzly's face. He ran forward, pointed his longrifle and pulled the trigger.

Then it all went black.

CHAPTER TWO

Sharka had wandered far away from the Cherokee village in her search for herbs and plants. She wasn't a medicine woman but began to learn about medicine when her daughter, Izusa, was so strangely born. She'd learned how to treat common illnesses rather than ask for help and bring any attention to the child.

They'd come upon the grizzly bear as they'd roamed the woods on the slopes of the mountains. Sharka hadn't expected to meet up with a creature that should've been in hibernation. The bear had evidently woken early and now was hungry and definitely in a bad mood.

She knew that she shouldn't run – the grizzly would merely give chase and it could move faster than the wind. Yet what else was there to do other than stand here and wait to be eaten? Slowly, as the bear looked around and roared, she edged back and forced Izusa to crawl into the undergrowth.

'Don't move,' she ordered her child. 'Stay until the bear goes away.'

Izusa cried. It was the sound of mewing – more like a kitten than a child.

'Shush . . . shush,' Sharka whispered. She pushed the child, made her crawl even further into the undergrowth, and prayed to the spirits that they'd protect her daughter.

Then it seemed her prayers were answered.

A young man ran towards the bear.

He screamed and waved his arms wildly. Then he turned his head and started to shout at her. She understood his words.

'Get down. Protect your head with your arms. Play dead.'

Sharka nodded and then shouted towards Izusa again. 'Don't move. Don't come out until the bear has gone.'

Then, as the man had ordered, she lay, head covered, her feet anchored into the ground. She turned her head slightly to watch the fight between the man and bear.

The man ran into the centre of the bear as if it was a cave – then she heard the sound of a rifle shot. She saw the bear collapse with the man underneath.

Then there was nothing but silence.

After it had been at least an hour since the last roar of the bear, she crawled into the undergrowth to join her daughter.

Later, when Stone opened his eyes, he spat the fur and blood from his mouth. The shot had found its mark and now, when he tried to move, he found that he was under the bear. The grizzly held him in a deadly embrace and for a while, all he could do was take its warmth until he had enough energy to wriggle his way out.

Fortunately, as he fell, he'd rolled to avoid the full weight of the bear. As he crawled out, he looked around for the young woman. There was no sign of anyone else.

'Let's hope there weren't two grizzly bears,' Stone said. He looked down at the fallen creature. 'Although I don't think you're pack animals like wolves or bison.'

Stone pushed the grizzly on to its back.

The beast was heavy. It wasn't easy or quick. Finally he eased it over with ropes secured to its right front and rear paws, wedged his packsack under its back and pulled. It acted as a fulcrum and pitched the bear over.

'Now you're dead, I best make use of you,' he said.

He took a long, sharp boning knife and made an incision from its neck to right between its lower legs and then two more incisions from paw to paw.

'Like skinning a rabbit, only bigger.' He chortled as he swiped at a couple of flies interested in what he was up to. 'Best hurry though, don't want anything bigger to come and see what I'm up to.'

Though he was quick, Stone took a couple of hours to get the fat and flesh from the hide. The most difficult thing to do was to cut around the pads of the feet to the edge of the hairline. In the end, he cut off the feet and pulled the claws to make a necklace later.

As he'd shot the grizzly through the mouth, there wasn't much of the head to preserve. He cut then pulled the fur from its face and over the back of its head.

He held it up to admire. The fur would make a good cover at night for the winter. He sprinkled all the salt he had, only a couple of pounds, over the inside of the skin, rolled it and placed it in a bag taken from his back pack.

Stone left all but a few sizeable chunks of red meat behind and continued on his journey.

'Those wolves and coyotes gonna have a party,' he said. 'They'll soon clear up this fat, and gristle, and innards.'

He'd placed a good pile of meat in another sack, and

hoisted it up a tree. He had a feeling that the woman was watching him. He hoped she'd have the sense to retrieve the meat.

Two pairs of large eyes followed the actions of Mayle Stone.

At first Sharka had believed the man to be dead. She held her daughter Izusa close to her and prayed that he'd killed the grizzly bear before the creature crashed down and crushed him. It had certainly surprised her to see the man crawl from underneath the grizzly. As he stood and looked around, she saw he was little more than a youth. Tall, certainly, but had yet to build the muscular bulk of a man.

The young odd child now looked at her mother in askance. The child was much older than people surmised. Izusa was as bright as a diamond and nine years old.

After they watched the man skin the grizzly, take the fur and some of the rich red meat with him, Sharka and Izusa returned to the Cherokee village.

Sharka's saviour became a legend.

She led her partner, Big Heart, and a few other braves, back to the spot of the bear fight. However, the scraps of bear left on the ground had been taken and predators had even licked the grass of blood. Then she pointed to the rope in the tree which when pulled lowered a considerable amount of meat for them.

'I do think he left it for us,' Sharka said.

'Maybe,' Big Heart replied. 'If he was coming back for it, well, it was ill-prepared.'

'He didn't look a coyote,' Sharka said. 'He was only young but if not for him, I and my daughter would be dead. I think it's a present.'

'Then the gods will look after him,' Big Heart said. 'And tonight we'll have a feast in his honour. We shall name the young man Grizzly Bear.'

CHAPTER THREE

Mayle Stone's gaze caught sight of a magnificent white wolf in the distance. The creature, one of the most despised and feared, howled.

'You lost your pack, wolfie?' Stone murmured. 'Too bad for you, but good for me.'

He'd already decided the fur would make a good deal of money. He got off his horse and tucked its reins under a large stone. Stone patted its hide as the animal's lips and muzzle gathered food that would've torn a man's mouth to shreds. He left it to graze on the wild grass and then picked up a small, white, soft down feather fallen from the breast of a bird. He held it up and watched as it floated down. It drifted over to the left side and it decided his approach to the wolf. He didn't want the beast to get a scent of him. Stone was now an experienced hunter, who'd lived off the land for many years.

When he was near enough to see the individual hairs of its topcoat, he lifted his longrifle, aimed, and fired. One flat crack of a rifle shot and the wolf was down. Stone grinned – his ma always said he could shoot a nut out of a squirrel's teeth at a hundred paces and never muss his whiskers – and this fine beast was an easier target than a squirrel.

17

He walked over to the wolf and then cursed. In his haste to get the fur he'd missed an obvious fact. It was a female with swollen teats on its underbelly. Cubs would be around somewhere, waiting for their mama to return. He reckoned he ought to follow its tracks and find the cubs otherwise they'd die within hours. Either the cold weather would freeze them in their den or hunger would finish them off.

And why waste such soft pelts?

Stone had little time to reflect on the situation because he heard the zip of an arrow. He looked down and saw it had pierced the ground between his feet. An angry snarling Indian jumped out of nowhere, it seemed to Stone, and confronted him.

'Pale Face, that is my wolf.'

There'd been no noise as the Indian touched the ground. Stone moved his gun slowly towards the man but kept the barrel low. In his belt he had a knife, which he believed better for hand-to-hand combat than any gun.

'You ought to shout out, to warn a fella,' Stone complained. 'You could get yourself killed with those damn moccasin feet.'

Stone returned the Indian's stare but kept his expression bland. This was a Cherokee. He knew the Cherokee Indians didn't hunt wolves because they believed their wolf brothers would hunt them down to exact revenge for the slain beast. The wolf was revered, however, so the kudos a wolfskin would bring was immeasurable.

Whether the Indian was speaking the truth or not, to call him a liar could only have one consequence – it would result in the death of one or the other of them. Mayle Stone had made his home in the mountains and knew every nook and cranny, every animal and every Indian band that lived there. However, he believed the young man's assumptions couldn't go unchallenged. The only way to live together was for everyone to respect each other and to just hand over the wolf hide to this young brave, wouldn't earn it.

'I don't see where your arrow has made a mark in its hide.' He pointed over to the small neat hole in the wolf's head. 'Looks like a bullet to me.'

The youngster's expression changed. His frown deepened. Stone was convinced he knew he was in the wrong but the eyes were fixed with the look of pure green envy.

'I was after a deer,' he explained. 'It was the noise you made which caused him to fly away.'

The explanation had a ring of truth. He was not stalking the wolf, his quarry was the deer. However the situation was, as Stone read it, the youngster wanted the valued fur in compensation. He also knew a rebellious young brave when he saw one. On his belt, tied around his breechcloth, hung several scalps. One of which looked as if the blood had only recently dried and Stone imagined that if you popped the clots, viscous red blood would emerge. A large knife, used frequently, Stone guessed, also decorated the Indian's attire.

As he took in this picture, Stone felt the young brave's searing gaze. His knowledge of hot-headed braves had taught him to take it slow and easy and not return any perceived hostility. He refrained from any quick movements and although he kept his gun barrel pointed downwards, he didn't let it go. Stone knew he had to manage things so it didn't escalate from an awkward situation into a minor war. He rubbed at his beard and considered the matter. A white fur was valuable, but so was his life. True, he could kill the youngster but he'd have to explain the death to his brothers. He wanted to continue to live here in the same peaceful manner as before. He bent forward, slowly, pulled the arrow from the ground and handed it back.

'We could do a deal that benefits us both,' Stone said. The brave visibly relaxed. Stone held up his hand in a friendly gesture. 'I'm Mayle Stone. I am honoured to have Cherokee blood in my veins.'

'I've heard of you. We call you Grizzly Bear.'

Stone nodded to acknowledge the compliment. The story of his fight with a grumpy grizzly bear had travelled far and wide over the last six years. Now he considered the tale to be grossly exaggerated. In retrospect, the bear barely out of hibernation had been an easy kill.

'Thank you,' he replied.

'I am Lightfoot of the Cherokees,' he said. 'You killed the wolf, Grizzly Bear, keep it.'

He spoke the words as if he'd given Mayle Stone a present. Stone accepted graciously but then returned the compliment.

'I'd like to offer it to you,' he said. 'If you'd fired the arrow before my shot startled the deer, you would have killed your prey.'

Lightfoot smiled like the youngster he was, about thirteen summers, but then remembered his rank.

'I accept,' he said. 'Now I owe you and I will send a present to your home.' He bent down, picked up the wolf and slung it over his shoulders as if it were a mere bag of feathers, not an eighty-pound animal.

Mayle Stone watched him go. He was indeed light-footed – as before, his steps made no sound on the mountain pathway.

It felt as if an ethereal moment had touched him as the figure disappeared from view to be replaced by swirls of morning mist. Then Stone suddenly became aware of the noises, birds and animals, in the pine forest and returned to reality and the other job he had to do.

The wolf was a mother. There were cubs nearby. He used his well-honed instincts of a hunter to locate them. He kept his eyes open as he glanced around to make sure the male wolf was not around. They were surprisingly strong creatures and judging by the size of the female, the male would be enormous and definitely stronger. They had teeth adapted for stabbing and crunching bones. He shuddered and tried not to imagine his thigh gripped between its massive jaws. Yet the female wolf had been howling as if she'd lost her pack. Perhaps the pack had gone hunting. He scanned the area, cautious of the dangerous situation he could be in.

In a very short time, he came across a place where the cubs could be. He dug them out – one black and two light grey cubs appeared. He aimed his gun to shoot them but then one of the grey cubs looked up at him. He seemed to find it difficult to still a soft spot in his heart and decided to let fate dictate the answer to their future. Their eyes were still blue and he reckoned the cubs were large enough to survive without complete dependence on their mother. He picked up the three and placed them in his gunny bag. After he'd shot a couple of rabbits and a small deer, he strapped them on to his muscular Pinter horse, and headed back to his mountain cabin.

His horse was a very quiet animal. Not much spooked his horse. It had powerful hindquarters for galloping, but also the strength and fortitude to pull itself through the deepest snow. He'd worked hard to purchase the young mare and bought it with furs.

Stone's kill hadn't been too far from the cabin and the return journey took barely forty minutes. He slapped his horse's neck and whispered as he encouraged it to gallop, 'We've had a good trip. Let's get home before dusk and I'll find some roots for you.' The horse whinnied as if it understood the promise.

When Stone tipped the cubs out on to the hay of the lean-to, only two still moved. He picked up the dead cub and placed it alongside a pile of furs he'd yet to finish cleaning. He listened to the other two mewing cubs and put a bucket under the cow he kept for milking. A couple of squirts half filled a shallow container and then he knelt down and moved the wolf cubs' heads towards it. The black cub stuck out its tongue and started to lap contentedly. Stone had to put milk on his fingers and force the other one to suck.

'Don't think you'll last the day,' he said.

The greedier cub fixed a stare on his brother as if in agreement with Mayle Stone. It lapped the precious milk until it dribbled back out of its mouth. Stone got some meat from his cooking pot, chewed it to a pap and fed them. They ripped into the mush and then swallowed.

'I'm sure glad you've reached that stage. My old cow needs another calf 'cause I've had trouble lately to squeeze half a cup of milk from it.' He looked at the animals. 'Stray wolves, or stray anything else are well down the pecking order when it comes to food.' He rubbed his belly. 'Darn well got to feed myself now, or I'll die of starvation.'

Yet Stone found the wolf cubs company at night. In the daytime he watched them at play. They fought like dogs. They practised jumping at each other as if catching prey. Occasionally, outside, he put a live rabbit in front of them. Sometimes it escaped. Most times the two wolves shared rabbit supper.

'That's right, learn to hunt. I won't be able to keep up with your appetites soon.'

After several weeks, curiously, it was the darker pup who seemed to take on the role of alpha male. The now white one had the habit of fading into the background but when it looked as if it had almost disappeared into the snowy vista, it attacked and caught its prey by sleuth.

'I reckon you're a survivor, too,' Stone said.

CHAPTER FOUR

Spring arrived. Stone came out of his log cabin to wash in the nearby lake. He spoke to the two wolves, Moon and Dark Star, that scrambled around his feet.

'I reckon some folks might call me queer but I like to clean up every couple of months – apart from deepest winter, that is.'

He stretched his arms, stood on tiptoes and breathed deeply.

'My good god, do I stink that much?' The question was rhetorical as he sniffed under his armpits. 'That comes of being in a cabin for months with the odour of stew and smoke and sweat and farts.' He laughed.

He guessed that after only just four months trapped in the snow bound cabin, he was in danger of becoming crazy. Why, he'd even given his wolves names, but they suited the colour of their beautiful coats. The snow still decorated the surrounding land but the horse, mules and wolves were running around and enjoying the freedom. Even the cow swished its tail and stamped its hoofs.

He pulled at his jacket and pants. 'I reckon these could do with a beating.'

He stripped down to his long johns and shivered.

No going back now.

After he shook and beat the cowhide pants and jacket

with a stick, he hung them over the branches of a pine tree to air. He used the same stick to break the thin ice that covered the water. He looked in.

'It's clear and bright and I bet it's certainly cold,' he said. 'No time for dipping the toes!' He held his shirt between his hands and dived.

'Aheeee!'

The cold took his breath away. His lungs were mere pancakes as he dove down into the depths. The surface of the water was calm for several minutes then he surfaced again. He stared as if he was seeing things when he came up for air. His body filled with oxygen and made him light headed. It looked as if two people were standing by the water's edge. He shook his head, blinked the water out of his eyes then unconvinced, he dived under again. Eyes wide open, he watched the fish, preserved from the coldest weather by the blanket of ice, swim around. He grabbed out at a fish's tail but it wasn't going to be the catch of the day because it slipped through his fingers like spreading grease on a fire. The fish turned and blinked twice. It seemed to be enjoying the sport before it weaved rapidly past and away.

He surfaced again. His shirt bobbed at his side in protest at being plunged into the icy water. The two figures he'd believed were merely a figment of his imagination were still there when he broke the surface again. They were as quiet as pine trees on a still day.

'What on earth?'

As he focused he recognized the young man. It was Lightfoot, the young brave to whom he'd given the wolf-skin. A girl, who seemed to be a strange little creature, stood by his side.

He wondered why the wolves hadn't warned him of the uninvited visitors but it seemed the reason was that the pair cowered and growled by the side of the lake, their gaze fixed on the man who wore their mother's skin as a robe.

Stone swiftly grabbed his soft chamois leather sheet and wrapped it around his body like a skirt because his long johns clung to him like a second skin. The girl fixed her gaze towards the ground, which, Stone thought, was good in the circumstances. He didn't want to offend but they'd invaded his private space. Two seconds later, he'd slipped on the jacket he'd hung from the tree branch, pushed his feet into boots and walked over towards them.

'I hope I didn't offend. I didn't intend to greet you un-shucked,' he said. He held up his hand in greeting. 'Good to see you again, Lightfoot.'

'I take no offence, Grizzly Bear,' the Indian replied. 'My name is now He With A Wolfskin.'

'Greetings, He With A Wolfskin.' Mayle Stone then looked at the girl. 'You've brought a friend?'

'This is my half-sister, Izusa.' Stone nodded a greeting. 'She is yours,' the Indian said. 'She has always been yours.'

'What do you mean?'

'The woman you saved.' Stone frowned. The young man's next words explained it. 'This is her daughter. Izusa stood by her side when the grizzly attacked. You now have Izusa as your woman.'

'Is that so. . . ? No. I mean, thank you, but I can't accept er . . . er . . . Issa?'

'Izusa. Name means white stone.' The young Indian laughed. 'My debt for the fur is repaid.'

'She's a young girl,' Stone protested.

'She has seen fifteen summers,' He With A Wolfskin answered. Then he didn't wait to hear any other protests. He squeezed the girl's hand, turned on his heels and disappeared as silently as he'd come. Izusa still looked down at the ground. She didn't move a muscle or say a word.

26

'You must go back to your village. You're not a thing to be bartered. You can't stay here.'

Only then did she look up. Her eyes opened as wide as full moons and had the colour of moons. Disconcerted by her appearance, he stepped back. Distressed by his reaction, she threw herself at his feet. Stone tried to act nonplussed as he attempted to get her to move away.

'Look, I gotta get a shave,' he said. 'You and your brother interrupted my ablutions.' She paused from locking her arms around his feet and looked at him almost as if he'd given her a reprieve. He squashed her hopes immediately. 'I tell you, I can't be having a crazy girl about. I will take you back myself.'

He was sure she'd ignored the last part of his sentence because at the mention of a shave, she jumped up and grabbed hold of his shaving kit, pulled his hand and started to drag him back towards the lake. The two wolves growled softly as their gaze followed the antics of the pair.

Stone, unsure what else to do, tolerated her actions for a while. She unbuttoned his jacket, but when she tried to unwind his chamois leather wrap, he stopped her.

'There's some things a man can do his self.'

He took the shaving kit away from her, however, before he could stop her, she'd found another chore. She hung his shirt on the tree to dry and gathered his pants and jacket.

'Those are clean already,' he protested.

Then he shut up as she beat the lice from the seams with a stone. As he lay by the waterside watching his clothes dry in the heat of the spring sun, the girl disappeared. The situation troubled Stone; to him she looked merely a girl, whatever her brother had said. Why, his twenty years meant he was far too old for her. As he considered what action to take, he knew he was in a quandary.

'To take back a gift is an insult,' he murmured, to the wolves.

They had been quiet for the last couple of hours, looking at Stone and then Izusa. They lay their heads on his torso and he contemplated his options.

'Don't think I got many,' he told them. 'I've lived in these mountains, tolerated by the Indians because, like them, I take nothing from the land but what I need to survive. And of course, a drop of their blood flows in mine.'

The wolves looked in Izusa's direction again. She'd gone into Stone's hut and had turfed out his things and taken a brush to the floor before shaking down and airing the bedding.

'Life will change if the Cherokee become my enemy.'

He wasn't ignorant of the animosity between the settlers and the Indians. He knew the feuding between them caused massacres on both sides. He'd considered himself immune from all that. He looked towards the log cabin. Inside, he saw Izusa hunched over a fire and could smell coffee and food.

'I reckon life's gonna change, regardless of what I decide.' He stood up and the wolves followed. 'Perhaps we can reach a compromise,' he said.

He took out a pallet, covered it with a straw mattress and the bear fur. 'You sleep here.'

Izusa smiled. He thought he saw a look of relief shine in her eyes.

Every day, Stone watched the young girl who'd appeared, out of nowhere, as payment for a good deed. When she'd lived with him for a couple of months, he thought he'd tell her she had no need to be so shy. Izusa never spoke, just nodded, smiled and then looked at the floor.

He took his opportunity one particular day when she'd cooked, cleared away the dishes and set about darning clothes, and he'd sat by her. She looked like a bird ready to fly away but he held her hand to stop her jumping up and away from him. Panic filled her face, her eyes wide as she looked at the large bed and then her gaze dropped to the floor as if resigned to the worst. He watched tears well up and splash on to the shirt she darned. Still holding her hands in his hand, he reached up and turned the downcast face towards him gently with his fingers.

She smiled at him.

'Why don't you speak to me?' This comment brought more tears, however, this time she didn't look away. 'You understand my words?' he asked. She nodded. 'Tell me,' he insisted.

She opened her mouth.

He let her go.

She reeled away at his reaction. She ran out into the wilderness. At first he thought she might have gone back to the Cherokees – but then surmised that the disgrace of his rejection would mean exile for Izusa from her people; it would be a death sentence. They must have considered her a burden, which was why the Indian brave had been more than happy to make a present of her to pay his debts.

Stone found her halfway up the mountains. She turned to look at him. For a moment he saw an unearthly quality about her, as if she was enveloped in a magical aura. He stared at her and briefly, he saw her as the others had – a girl from another world.

He held out his hand, she responded to the gesture and followed him back to the cabin.

He disappeared for a few days afterwards to take time to think and then finally he made up his mind. She couldn't go back to the Cherokee. He'd decided he would like a companion. Yet he didn't want a forced relationship. Whether she was a girl or a woman, he would protect her and nothing more.

When he returned he said nothing. The next morning, he walked a little way up the trail with his axe and mallet and walked into a clearing. He did this the next morning and the following morning and every morning after that, and did not return until late. Then curiosity got the better of her and she started to follow. She watched as he constructed a simple cabin. He pointed to her and then to the cabin.

'This is yours. You'll feel safe here. It doesn't matter if you can't speak.' Disbelief washed over her face. 'Hell, I know lots of men who'd be happy to pay a premium for a woman who couldn't say a dang word!'

Izusa stayed in the cabin for a while and then came back to him. She sat on the big bed but he shook his head.

'No, we will wait. Then we'll go to the preacher and marry. That is if you want to?' Stone's cheeks flushed. He'd proposed to the young woman. She smiled and nodded – the tenseness of her body dissipated.

He took it as agreement to the plan. He pointed to the bed she'd used when she first arrived.

'If you want to sleep here sometimes, use the pallet bed.'

Stone thought of her as a child.

As the first year together merged into the next, they became relaxed in each other's company.

Then Stone noted a change. Izusa seemed less gawky and awkward – less prone to knocking pots and pans or falling over anything and everything.

'Must have known you were going to move in when I added space to the cabin with the stables on the side.' He laughed. 'Reckon everyone's had too much good food. Even you're getting fat, Izusa!' He laughed again and prodded her belly but she blushed and turned away.

A day or so later, soon after his comment about the change in Izusa, he saw her bathing at the edge of the lake. Like Venus, she emerged from the water, and displayed her beauty. The scrawny child's angular shape had gradually softened into the roundness of a young woman. He knew Izusa slipped out at night, when the moon was new to bathe. This time, perhaps because she assumed he'd be away hunting, she'd ignored her own rule of secrecy. He'd wanted to surprise her with a fine deerskin he hoped she'd fashion into a shift. Now he couldn't reveal his presence and hung back.

His mouth dropped open in surprise at the white hair, which framed her face and hung below her shoulders. Her skin was so light – almost translucent. He gasped at the beautiful sight.

'An apparition,' he murmured.

He squinted his eyes, as if perhaps it was the effect of the bright sun but no, even when a cloud briefly shadowed the sun, she still appeared light. He turned away. He didn't make his presence known – not yet.

Later, when he appeared again, everything was as it was before. Stone knew a change had occurred and it was something, which couldn't be hidden, unlike the hair and skin she'd carefully darkened with a vegetable dye.

CHAPTER FIVE

Jon Rudyman stepped back into the shadows of the fort. He watched the young woman. To him, the man who escorted her into Fort St Vrain looked old enough to be her pa and yet the way he grasped her hand, put his arm around her shoulder or glanced at her, no pa would ever do that in public.

Then he took a second look at the couple.

He reckoned the man by her side wasn't that old but rough and coarsened; his skin leathered and aged by the harsh climate. A climate that was too hot, too dry or too cold. The weather in Colorado offered little comfort to a man at times.

A man who lived off the land paid a price. In Rudyman's opinion, it took his youth, health and sanity. Rudyman was fond of repeating this phrase as he bummed around: 'looking for business opportunities.' No one commented. It was well known at the fort that Rudyman took more than he gave.

At this moment he wanted that young woman – no, she was only a girl. She was a squaw, but all the better, he thought. They were 'earthier' and more 'natural' than the insipid white women. His eyes clouded as he watched the girl. He imagined himself alone with her. His hand moved towards his belt as if the visions threatened to spiral into action.

Then he heard the man speak.

'You're a piece of sunshine captured in a moment.'

He saw her smile and gaze at him.

Rudyman's teeth gnashed together. It made him angry.

'What have you got to be happy about, girl?' he murmured as he continued to stare. 'In a few years, your youth will be marred by wrinkles as well. Perhaps I ought to give you something to remember in your old age.'

Almost as if she'd become aware of something, she looked towards the shadows.

'My god! What's wrong with her eyes?'

The words were spoken louder than he intended. It caught the attention of a man walking on the boardwalk nearby. He stopped and spoke.

'There's naught wrong except she's one of those Albinos. The man next to her, that's Mayle Stone. You'd best focus on him. He looks like a broom handle and you'd think he'd blow away in a snowstorm, yet story goes he was only about fourteen when he killed a grizzly. In fact, the Cherokees call him Grizzly Bear even tho' he looks nothing like a bear. It's an honour they've bestowed on him. An' that Indian? Why, it's said he's gonna marry her, proper, with a preacher.'

The speaker was an old man who chawed tobacco, too much of it, as a black ulcer on his upper lip testified.

'What you telling me all that for?' Rudyman asked. 'I don't want to know the man's life story. You ought to be careful what you say and who you say it to, old man.'

The man carried on chawing and scratched at his crotch like he needed to relieve an itch but perhaps as much out of habit as his hair was slicked back clean from the washhouse.

'The name's Lee Bandy. I always believe that maybe a word of caution is useful sometimes. I can tell you, I don't take much to Indians meself, but that one's as sweet as anyone I've ever met. Mayle Stone, well, he gives me the odd rabbit or two when he comes to the fort. Treats me better than most. So when I see a man dribbling over his missus-to-be, I think it's my business to say something.'

Jon Rudyman frowned. 'I'm just passing the time, old man. I keep myself to myself. I suggest you do the same.'

Under the glare of Rudyman's cold eyes, Lee Bandy stepped back. Rudyman frowned.

Would he warn Stone about the comments he'd heard?

As the old man turned to walk away, Rudyman stopped him. He put a hand on Bandy's shoulder. 'I was rude. Let me make amends and allow me to introduce myself. Let me buy you a drink.'

Bandy paused. The fella sounded apologetic. He smiled.

A drink was a drink, no matter who bought it.

'Thankee, son, I think I might. A bath always takes it outta me. Damn ridiculous idea soaking in water more than once a year. There's a good cantina back-a-ways.'

He pointed to a row of shacks across from whence he'd appeared. It was dark and private. Rudyman's lips pressed together in an attempt to suppress a grin.

'That's as good a place as any, Bandy,' he said.

Izusa looked into the shadows yet she saw nothing. She shuddered and pulled a blanket, which she used as a shawl, closer. As Mayle Stone went about the business of bargaining for supplies, she always stayed with the horse and mules. Stone traded the furs they'd brought down the mountains to Fort Vrain. She wasn't allowed in the buildings of the fort, and although Mayle said he'd speak to the

34

commanding officer, she'd declined his help.

She recalled what an officer had said to Stone. 'There are ladies at the fort and they will be offended seeing an Indian woman acting up as a white man's wife.' Stone argued that Indian men traded at the fort but the officer was adamant. 'They have learned that such things are necessary, but no offence,' the officer looked at Izusa, 'this would be a step too far.'

Izusa waited outside the store. Quietly. Patiently. She'd learned the art of fading into the background. She thought back to her childhood spent mostly alone – away from other children. As she became older, she'd tried to find a place within the tribe. It was then Sharka told how white men had set upon her and how later she'd given birth to a deformed child – Izusa.

'It was pure luck that a handsome brave fell in love with me.' Sharka sighed.

Izusa tried to shake the bad thoughts away. Life had moved on. Moon growled. The sound, low in his throat, warned her of danger. She stepped nearer to the wolf and looked for the reason for his reactions. She saw a man. She wrinkled her nose in a display of distaste as the smell of whiskey preceded him. Izusa stepped between the horse and mules and signalled the wolf to stay silent. The footsteps stopped next to her. She shivered as his gaze went up and down her body and she lowered her eyelids as if to shield and protect herself. His laugh sounded harsh, as brittle as shards of glass on a path.

'You lonely, little girl?' She ignored him. Moon growled. The man kept his distance. 'Well, look the other way if you want but I'll tell you this – you and me are gonna be friends some day soon,' he whispered.

She gasped, alarmed at his words, then glanced up as he continued on his way.

Izusa moved towards Stone when he returned with their supplies. She put her hand on his arm as if to be reassured he was there before she helped him to load the mules. He raised his eyebrows but she smiled sweetly. There was never any conversation between them but instinctively both communicated by touch and signs.

However, how could she tell him about a stranger who made her shudder and fear for her safety?

A gust of biting wind reminded them that winter wasn't far away. They worked together to load the mules and stock up before the snows arrived. Izusa glanced back as the fort receded in the distance and eventually so did the memory of the man.

Izusa, convinced she'd tied the sack of flour securely, paced around the mules and then moved down the trail. Yet there it was, as she looked back to where they'd trailed from the fort, sprayed out in a cobweb of white flour. It had painted the mountain rocks as the sack flapped open in the wind. Stone called out to her. Izusa instinctively dropped to her knees, her hands clasped together and her mouth open in a soundless cry. Stone put his hand on her shoulder.

'Don't fret,' he said. 'I'll go back down and collect some more.'

He removed the few things they'd put in the saddle bags and left her to unload the mules. She motioned him to wait and pointed to the cabin and to have a bellyful of hot food.

'No. I'll go straightaway. I'll be back with you soon.'

Izusa had no time to ponder what had gone wrong, she had stores to unload and stash away from both winter weather and winter creatures such as bears and coyotes. The mules she took to their shelter and made sure they were fed, watered and the door locked against predators. It wasn't really necessary at the moment – the wildlife was still supplied with plenty of food and had no need to prey on bony, tough skinned mules until they were desperate with hunger. It was midnight before Izusa finished the chores. She fell on to the pallet bed and tried to sleep. Moon curled up beside her.

CHAPTER SIX

To ask questions about the how and why of the incident would only distress Izusa, Stone believed, because from her actions she blamed herself for the mishap. He'd examined the sack and found it'd been slashed in several places – just enough to let the flour seep slowly out. Any faster and they would have noticed the stuff blowing around them.

'It might have been worse to give her something else to worry about,' he muttered. 'I'll tell her about my suspicions later.'

Stone gritted his teeth and remounted his horse. He made his way down the Cherokee Trail and Dark Star followed closely. Stone treated the wolf as a dog and trained him to walk to heel and hunt with him. Dark Star in turn worshipped Stone as a leader of the pack, which consisted of Stone, the woman and Moon. Stone believed he could make it back to the fort by nightfall but warned Izusa it could be the following day before he returned. Initially he'd thought of waiting 'til the morrow to leave but decided the weather was on the turn and it was best to replace the flour immediately.

He soon came upon his goal, Fort St Vrain. According to folks who'd been in these parts for years, the low open building had started off as a church but bits had been added as the gold rush increased the population. The army too had increased in size and brought their wives and 'laundry women' with them. They were adding buildings to house their men and 'followers' after people in the surrounding areas had suffered Indian attacks. The Indians objected to being shoved off the land because in their psych, there was enough for everyone to live comfortably and couldn't understand why the settlers wanted to 'claim' it.

It was always noisy in the store but today, it caught him unawares when he opened the door and met a cacophony of sound mingled together with the smell of strong coffee, beer and stale farts. Dark Star growled and started to follow on Stone's heels.

'Wait outside,' he commanded. Dark Star obeyed but his answering growl expressed his dislike of the order.

Stone took stock of his surroundings. His head was full of conflicting notions. Did any of these men in here have a grudge against him? Who'd leave the warmth of the log burner to slash a bag of flour?

The storekeeper was the only one to notice his arrival.

'Thought you'd been and gone,' Bert Wilkins said.

'Well, now I've come back,' Stone answered.

'Glad you've left that mangy mongrel outside,' Wilkins observed.

'You want to say that to him?' Stone laughed at the man's discomfort and then added, 'It seems like a hullabaloo is going on in here.'

'The talk is of Lee Bandy's death,' Wilkins said.

Stone shrugged. 'I recall the old man. Nice fellow. Always drunk. Did he drown in a vat of beer?'

Wilkins frowned. 'No. There's talk of murder.'

Stone placed the empty flour bag on the counter. 'That

so? Well, I've come about this.'

The puzzled storekeeper scratched at his bald head. 'An' I don't know what yer expect me to do about it.'

Then his attention was distracted as the door opened and a passel of fresh air filtered through the store. Wilkins looked past Mayle Stone and watched as a couple of women, dressed in outfits of satin and lace, which had seen better days, entered the store. They looked the type of women who accompanied the soldiers from fort to fort.

'I see. Left your squaw at home? So you want to get your collar starched by the laundry women?'

Wilkins chuckled but the joke didn't go further than his lips as Stone ignored the women with painted faces and warned the storekeeper, 'I think you need to be careful what you say about my "squaw".' He pointed to the flour bag again. 'I need to replace this,' he said. 'I'd prefer one that didn't have the same fault. I reckon you owe me a discount, Bert.'

The storekeeper frowned and picked up the coarse cotton bag as if it were contaminated. 'How do I know you ain't done this. . . ?'

He didn't finish his sentence. Stone grabbed him by the collar and hauled him across the counter. 'You accusing me of cheating?'

Wilkins was in no position to point out that Stone had virtually accused him of the same thing. He coughed and spluttered as he shook his head. Stone loosed his grip and the man slid slowly to his feet again behind the counter. He shook his shoulders and straightened his shirt.

'Probably an accident,' he looked at Stone again and blenched before adding, 'or most possibly, a defect with the bag.'

Mayle Stone wasn't a giant of a man, the opposite, in fact. He looked like a tall stick but he was muscular and tough. Not many men would come off best in a fight with him.

'I'll give you a discount, ten per cent, and call it quits.'

Stone's stare didn't falter. 'Fifty per cent,' he said.

Wilkins gulped. 'Fifteen per cent'

'Forty-five.'

'Forty.'

Stone spat into his palm and offered a handshake to the storekeeper. 'Agreed,' he said.

'Of course, I can't do it until Tuesday morning, you took the last an' I'm waiting on another supply.'

Mayle Stone frowned. 'You sure you got none out back?'

Wilkins shook his head. 'Nothing,' he said.

Sunday was nearing its end. He'd have to trek back home and come almost straight back again to be here for Tuesday. Stock didn't stay in store long. And he couldn't trust Wilkins to keep back anything he could sell for a hundred per cent and he reckoned the deal they'd made had robbed the storeman of his profit.

Jon Rudyman had watched the exchange. He approached as Stone pondered the best course of action.

'I think I could help you pass your time with some money in it for you,' he said.

Stone eyed the man. When a complete stranger approaches you, especially with offers of money, there was a need for caution. 'What d'you mean? I don't even know your name.'

'Name's Jon Rudyman.' Stone accepted the handshake from Rudyman's outstretched hand. 'I guess it sounds strange, but there's something for both of us if you can help me.'

'Mayle Stone,' he said. 'State your business.'

Stone didn't hold with prying but if you were approached first, you needed to know whether you were facing a rattlesnake or a skunk. Neither made good friends but one would kill you whereas the other would only cause a nasty smell. He observed that Rudyman's brows ran unbroken across his forehead so he looked as if he had a permanent frown. The left eye was green and the other brown and they tried to draw together for company. His thin lips didn't look as if they'd ever exercised a smile. Stone mentally pushed the thought away – a man couldn't help it if he weren't blessed with a pretty face.

'Let me buy you a drink, Mr Stone.' Rudyman looked towards the storekeeper who openly stared at the two men. 'Let's sit in that corner over there. I'd like to keep details private between us.'

Bert Wilkins spat on his shirtsleeve and used it to dust the counter furiously, as if only a spot of dirt concerned him.

The fact that Mayle Stone had returned to the fort held no surprise for Jon Rudyman. It hadn't taken a moment to stab at the flour sack, as he brushed past. In fact, he had to keep a grin from his face, because it was better than he'd anticipated; Stone was alone so he had only one problem to contend. Once they had a couple of glasses and a bottle of whiskey between them, Jon Rudyman unrolled a yellowed parchment. His grimy thumb stabbed at a spot on the map.

'This here is Yellow Rock mine,' he said. He moved his thumb slightly so Stone could see the black cross.

Stone looked and then blinked. 'So, I see a cross on a map. Is it hereabouts?'

'That's what I need to find out,' Rudyman explained. 'I was given this map when I helped a wounded man.

42

Unfortunately, it was too late to save him, but he gave me the map and said it wasn't too far from Deadman's Plate.'

In Mayle Stone's opinion, although he kept his thoughts private, Rudyman didn't have the look of a man who went round saving anyone.

'Yeah, I know Deadman's Plate, about twenty miles north of here,' he said. 'It's rugged country and near a valley called Devil's Gulch, is a place to avoid round there.'

'Why?' Rudyman asked.

'Full of places to trip you up. I knew a fella whose horse's leg got broken. They didn't make it back – found their skeletons years later.'

'You could say that about any place.'

'That's true. Although folks say they hear the man calling for help.'

Rudyman waved his hand, dismissing the idea of ghosts. He focused only on one idea. 'Could you take me there?' he asked. 'I tried twice and ended up in circles.'

'The land can be mighty unforgiving if you don't know the territory,' Stone agreed. He shook his head. 'Like to help but I've got supplies to take home.'

'I couldn't help but hear you'll be kicking your heels until Tuesday,' Rudyman said. 'Perhaps you could take me as far as Devil's Gulch and point me in the right direction. You'd be back here with time to spare.'

Mayle Stone pushed his glass away and went to stand up. 'I don't take to people organizing my time.'

Rudyman placed his hand over Stone's arm. 'This is a gold mine. You take me there and I promise to give you a share.' His mouth tried to move into a smile but, like Stone had guessed, it trembled as if it didn't know how. 'I'll make it so profitable you won't need to bargain with a storekeeper over the price of flour. You'll darn well be able to buy the store!'

Mayle Stone sat down. He looked at Rudyman and wondered how genuine the man was. The truth was, Stone believed, that if he told this story too many times to strangers, he'd probably end up dead and definitely minus the map.

'OK, I'll take you up those hills and show you how to make your way for the last few miles to where you reckon you'll find Yellow Rock mine,' he said.

'Thank you.' Jon Rudyman was on his feet as if ready to leave.

'We'll start out at daybreak,' Stone said.

'You're bringing that thing along?'

Rudyman showed no love of the huge black creature that waited at Stone's side.

'Yes. Got any problems with that?'

The wolf snarled at Rudyman.

'No. Just keep that thing away from me. Ain't natural to have a beast like that around.'

Flakes of snow slipped down their collars as the two men, together with the wolf, rode out.

'That sky looks ready to dump a whole lot of snow on us,' Stone commented. 'Let's hope we make it there, and back, without mishap.'

'All I want is to find that gold mine,' Rudyman said.

'You sure it exists? A lot of forged maps about.'

Rudyman brushed Stone's misgivings away. 'I feel in my bones I'm – I mean we – we're gonna strike lucky,' he said.

Again, Rudyman's lips couldn't style themselves into a smile but his manner was jaunty and Stone shrugged. He'd refused Rudyman's offer of a share in something he didn't reckon existed. He didn't want to get involved in this other than to pass the time until he could get his flour and go home. He hoped Izusa would guess he'd been delayed at the fort and not worry too much. She'd never show it, though; she kept her feelings wrapped away. As he rode alongside Rudyman, he thought of Izusa, a tiny, nervous creature, who'd become such an important part of his life.

CHAPTER SEVEN

Rudyman's voice brought Stone back to the present. He pushed his thoughts of Izusa to the recesses of his mind.

'What?'

'How far you reckon it'll be?' Rudyman asked again.

'Deadman's Plate is only a couple of miles away now. Then we'll look at your map again.'

Their sparse conversation lapsed into silence as the men continued their journey.

Rudyman watched Stone's surefooted horse plod on and began to think that maybe he'd take that as well. The mule he rode was a damn stubborn broken-winded beast and he'd be happy to leave it in exchange. Rudyman dragged his coat collar tighter around his neck and pulled his hat down over his ears and his neckerchief over his nose and mouth.

'I swear that north wind has changed direction and it's cutting across from the east,' he grumbled.

Either the wind blew away his words or perhaps Stone just ignored him because there was no reaction. Rudyman's mood turned foul as the wind even found its way through the hole in his left boot and clutched and scissored at his toes. He shook his foot to try and loosen its grip but merely allowed the cold air to filter up and turn his sock into what felt like an icy tourniquet. His heels cut into the mule's side but the creature seemed unaware and merely plodded on.

The thought of Stone's woman was the only thing that kept him warm and his saddle felt hot. Rudyman had only to close his eyes to bring to mind the large doe-like eyes, blush brown skin and tiny but voluptuous body. Even though slightly odd, she was better than anything else he'd seen this side of the Rockies. Saliva dribbled from his lips under the neckerchief and froze on his chin. His gloved hand brushed it away. The picture dissolved as he heard Stone call to him.

'Just over the top of this ridge and we can hitch our mounts and study that map o' yours.'

Rudyman nodded in response. His hand shifted to his half-cocked flintlock gun. As soon as the horses were hitched, he wouldn't waste another minute in the effort of friendly conversation.

Stone regretted this journey right from the start. The man had stunk of whiskey before they'd sat together in the cantina. He didn't think the man was drunk but he wasn't a stranger to the brew and its odour had settled into the fabric of his clothes, as did the short cigars he chewed rather than smoked. Then he looked at it another way. The other option would've been to kick his heels at the trading post until Tuesday. No, he reasoned as he came to the top of the final butt before Deadman's Plate, going on this goose chase at least passed the time of day.

'See that?' Stone pointed to the flat top mountain ahead. 'It's got a story to it—'

'Ain't interested in stories and the like,' Rudyman interrupted.

Stone continued as if Rudyman had not spoken. 'The

Indians tell the tale of a huge beast, such as had never been seen before, it was looking for food and came across a band of young Indian braves. The beast decided they'd make a tasty snack but they ran like the wind and called on their gods to protect them. The gods were in a foul mood that day, don't know why, but they looked upon the braves and thought they ought to have been able to fend off the beast. "You want help?" they asked and when the response was yes, the gods told them it was at a cost. Of course, the frightened braves were ready to promise anything and agreed. Suddenly the earth shook underneath them. What they call Deadman's Plate rose up. The beast and six of the braves were on it. To the other braves the gods said, "Now is your chance to flee." The braves on the mountain were served up to the beast on a plate.'

Rudyman squinted at the mountain as a rare glimpse of sun appeared and the sky caught its edge. A flash hurt his pupils as he concentrated on conjuring up the scene Stone had painted. He turned to avoid the sun's rays, saw Stone's grin, and frowned.

'You're making it up,' he growled.

Stone shrugged his shoulders. 'Just a tale I heard,' he said. 'I'd say we're a couple of hours away from that black cross on your map. Not that I know a deal about it. I've wandered these hills for years and I still make a new discovery every week. Perhaps your mine will be on that list.'

Rudyman scowled. His face said he had a notion Mayle Stone was funning him again and he didn't like it. Then Mayle Stone saw a clearing in the pine trees.

'That's a good point to rest up and work out the best route forward,' he said.

He beckoned Jon Rudyman to follow him.

Rudyman had got very little from Mayle Stone. The man

was tight-lipped about most things – except his scathing comments about the gold mine.

'Been plenty of finds hereabouts but none by Deadman's Plate.' The man laughed. 'Perhaps it's been swallowed up by that huge beast which could be hiding in Devil's Gulch now.'

Rudyman mirrored Stone's smile yet he could feel bubbles of anger rising up inside. He popped them one by one as he thought of Stone's Indian woman, squashed helplessly beneath his broad body. This kept the large smile creased over his face.

'Glad you can take a joke,' Stone said.

'Oh, yeah, I like a good joke,' Rudyman replied.

They sat near the small fire Stone had fashioned from dry twigs and bark kindled with a spark from his knife, and chewed on jerky and drank strong coffee. The two relaxed and chatted. Or as near as the two of them could ever come to that position. Rudyman kept his flintlock in his holster and Stone laid his longrifle by a flat stone that he'd perched on to use as a stool.

Rudyman did manage to wheedle out the information from Stone that it'd take several hours journeying north, back from the fort, to get home, and while it was threatening to snow here, where he lived the snow would already be on the ground. He'd always looked forward to going home to his cabin nestled amongst the trees off the Cherokee trail.

'Good to have a place to call your own,' Rudyman said. 'You're lucky.'

'Don't call it luck,' Stone replied. 'I left home – well, a house of sorts – it had three bark walls laid against a slab of rock an' topped with a sod roof. The door was an opening 'cause my pa couldn't sober up enough to fix one into it. When he died and another pa took his place, I decided it was time to go.'

'Seems we had the same sort of start,' Rudyman said.

Stone chewed harder on his piece of jerky and said nothing. He noticed Dark Star had wandered off. The lure of fresh meat in the form of rabbit or fawn had been too much to keep him by his master's side. A short time later, Rudyman threw the dregs of the coffee on the ground and added more wood to the fire.

'Time to bed down?' he suggested. 'I could take first watch. And tomorrow we'll find this mine.'

Stone nodded and drew his blanket over him and used his saddle as a pillow. A short time after, the tiredness took over and he closed his eyes.

Mayle Stone lay in a puddle of blood. After a vague amount of time – as the cold air chilled his skin and started to turn his insides to ice – he opened his eyes, slowly.

'What the . . . it feels like . . .'

He knew, instinctively, he had to move or risk freezing. He lifted his head. His saddle was gone. He grimaced.

'I think he's bashed my head in,' he moaned. He pushed his body into a sitting position but fell face down several times before he made it. 'I dunno what happened. . . .'

He tried to recall and frowned, one moment he been getting some shut-eye and the next. . . . Gingerly, he touched the back of his head. He quickly drew his hand away as it throbbed under his fingers. Silently he cursed his idiocy. How could he have trusted the man? Yet he had nothing to steal. His eyes glanced towards where they'd hitched the horses. Only one mount – a broken-winded mule – remained. Stone tried to stand, and winced with the pain of the action as he slipped over again. He looked up at the mule.

'It's one heck of a lot of trouble for a horse,' he said. 'Even my goddamn ears hurt at the sound of my own voice.'

Then the mule brayed and Stone again covered his ears with his hands.

It could've been days later, Stone thought, when he opened his eyes again. However, the sun had only moved a few degrees across the sky so the time could be measured in minutes or hours. He looked but couldn't see any of his belongings.

'That ornery cuss has took everything.'

Stone shook as he stood up and grabbed at a pine tree trunk. He touched his head again. There was no more blood.

'I reckon if I can get on that mule and head home, I'll have a fighting chance.'

As he thought of home, he had an uncomfortable feeling, like someone had walked over his grave. He reasoned that the bump to his head had brought fanciful thoughts to his mind. Jon Rudyman had no idea where he and Izusa lived. Or had he? His mind went over their brief conversation. He put the disturbing thoughts out of his mind completely.

'Whoa, Joe,' Stone said. He approached the mule cautiously. 'Don't know if your name is Joe but it suits you.'

The mule lifted its head and brayed as if happy at being called anything that didn't sound like a curse followed by a kick. Stone fashioned a bridle and bit with the rope that tethered it and slipped it over the mule's head, taking care to keep up a stream of chatter to calm the beast. It worked. Before the mule had time to resist, Stone climbed on its back and nudged forward in the direction of home.

'Don't know where that son-of-a-bitch master of yours

headed off but it ain't my concern . . . yet.'

He called for Dark Star but there was no replying howl to his whistle.

CHAPTER EIGHT

The sleep she longed for eluded Izusa. Endlessly she went over and over how the sack of flour could've been damaged. She recalled how there'd been a lot of hustle and bustle as they left. As they started to leave the fort, she'd heard the shout go up.

'Lee Bandy is dead!'

Quizzically she'd raised her eyebrows to ask Stone what it was all about but he hadn't heard and she couldn't explain.

Eventually Izusa gave up on sleep and got out of bed. She felt weak because she hadn't eaten and the solitude of her situation enveloped her like a dense blanket. Aware that she couldn't alter the loneliness she felt, she set about finding something to eat. She could prepare a meal to satisfy her hunger and it would be something for when Mayle Stone returned. She looked towards the fire. It was almost out. They needed fire. She placed dry grass to kindle the flames and sticks of wood on the top. Outside it had started to snow and a thin white blanket slowly covered the land that surrounded the cabin.

The following day she decided to do something.

She couldn't sit and wait for Stone to return. It was almost as if a sixth sense told her he might be in trouble.

She covered the stew, after taking a bowl for her sustenance, and then placed it to the side of the fire. If Stone returned while she was gone, he would find a warm cabin and food. It also left a signal that she was OK – that she'd prepared to leave and not drifted off without a plan.

Moon had a plan too – he followed his mistress.

The sun had yet to rise to bring the dawn and warmth when she set out. It was bitterly cold but she banked on the fact that if she could make good time then she'd return before the sun set on the homeward trail. Three quarters of the way to Fort St Vrain, she could see its black outline on the horizon.

The old trail running aside the Colorado Rockies served to connect the Arkansas and Platte rivers. Izusa's people called it the Cherokee trail, although throughout history it had many names. New settlers called it the Californian road. She could see where the ground had been rutted by the wheels of the provision wagons that brought supplies to the gold seekers and subsequently to the settlers. In her mind's eye she pictured the adventurers, the nomads, the fur trappers, the traders and occasionally the soldiers from the forts who walked or rode the trail over the years. At this time of year people scurried past, a brief nod in the direction of a stranger, because it was time to hole up at the fort or grab provisions and head home.

Izusa stopped at the fort gate, or rather, the soldiers stopped Izusa.

'You ain't welcome, squaw woman.'

Izusa sat and waited. She sat squarely at the gate. No one could move in or out with a wagon.

Eventually, as her nose turned pink then red with the fiercely cold breeze, which blew from the east, a young soldier took pity and let her through.

'Keep out of mischief,' he warned. He pointed to the wolf. 'And leave that thing outside.' Moon growled deeply from his chest. The soldier looked uncomfortable. Do I really want that wolf near me, he thought.

'OK. Keep it with you but make sure it's under control or it'll get shot.'

She went to Wilkins's store. The chatter of men sharing jokes, arguing over this and that and telling tales of valour went from ear splitting to silent as soon as she stepped into the store. Izusa ignored the stares, walked across the room and pointed to the flour. She placed a sack on the counter. Wilkins looked at the bag and shook his head.

'I ain't got naught to sell,' he said.

Izusa frowned. She placed some white rabbit skins by the bag. Wilkins folded his arms and shook his head again. Izusa added a small white fox fur to the pile. They both knew this was more than enough to fill the bag she held out, twice over and to overflowing.

'I ain't got naught to sell,' he repeated.

Wilkins received an encouraging cheer from one of the trappers heating his rear by the stove. A brief glance around the store told her there were no friendly faces in the place. She gathered up the sack as if aware she was unlikely to get any help at the store – either for flour or information about Stone's whereabouts. She shrugged her shoulders to show that it didn't bother her. She grabbed her things and walked back to the entrance of the store amidst the comments from the men.

'Ya sure know how to treat those Injun squaws, Wilkins.'

'They're no good for anything but to shack up with.'

'Better than a white woman in this neck of the woods. Used to the hard life. Do as they're tol'. And I believe that one don't talk.'

Outside, Izusa put her hands to her ears.

*

Izusa banged on the door of Second Lieutenant George Casey Peterson. Two soldiers stepped up and tried to get her to leave. She refused to move. She continued to bang on the door. Eventually Peterson opened it and shouted, 'What in tarnation is all this noise about?' He stood and stared at the woman. 'Oh goddamn! Do I know you? What do you want?'

She pointed to a sack and furs and then pointed again towards the general stores.

'Go and find out what's the matter over there, soldier,' he commanded.

Izusa grabbed hold of the soldier's arm and shook her head. She pointed at the Second Lieutenant.

The young soldier, Yem Jaegar, who'd let her into the fort, put his hand over his mouth as he tried to hide a smirk. 'Ahem, Lieutenant Peterson, I think she wants you to sort the problem out.'

Reluctantly, Lieutenant Peterson accompanied Izusa, together with the soldier, Jaegar, who seemed to think the whole episode a joke, but silenced his sniggers with a look from the lieutenant, to the general store. Inside the store, the sound of loud laughter seemed to shake the building. Once the soldiers appeared, the men's laughter stopped.

Wilkins stepped up to the counter immediately. 'What can I do for you, Lieutenant?'

'You can start by making my life a little easier, store-keeper,' he answered.

Wilkins frowned. 'Anything. What do you require?'

'I want you to serve this woman,' Lieutenant Peterson requested.

A few snorts of laughter greeted this remark and someone from a group of men around the log burner

56

offered his help. 'I can serve the little lady.'

Peterson glowered in the direction of the voice. 'Can I remind you that this is a fort, and as such, I am the law. Another funny comment and you'll find yourself in gaol.'

'Lieutenant, I would've served the woman if she'd have asked.'

Muffled chortles, thick as the smoke from all the cigars, filled the room. Wilkins's face turned white as he saw the gun in the lieutenant's grasp. He spluttered and took several moments to recover his composure again.

'Sorry, Lieutenant, you said that they weren't allowed inside the fort buildings. And I didn't think you'd want me to serve an Indian woman.'

'Let me decide the rules in this fort,' Lieutenant Peterson said. 'And if you don't hear them from me, don't invent your own.'

'No, siree,' Wilkins promised. 'So any of the Indian women are welcome at the fort?'

The lieutenant's face paled again and he lifted the gun towards the storekeeper. Wilkins reacted quickly and grabbed the sack from Izusa and half filled it before securing it with string.

'An' don't you get the sack ripped up this time. That man of yours, he came back, but we were out of flour. It was pure luck I got fresh stock before winter.' He directed the comment to Izusa but she frowned and shook her head as if refusing to accept any blame.

Izusa looked at the two men.

'Stone?' Her lips mouthed the word as she drew the name in the flour that had spilled on to the counter.

'No idea,' Lieutenant Peterson said.

Izusa again grabbed at Lieutenant Peterson's arm and he stepped back as if unsure of her action. Then he heard the men laugh.

'Want me to call your men to protect you?' Wilkins asked.

'I'm OK. Get back to your business of shortchanging your customers.' Wilkins's skin flushed and he lowered his eyes. 'Too near the truth, eh?'

Izusa pointed to the counter again. 'Stone?' Prodded the words written in the flour until they disappeared.

'He's gone. I suggest you return home as soon as you can.'

CHAPTER NINE

The rattle of pans as she prepared vegetables filled the cabin and broke the silence of the world outside. Then Moon's ears pricked up. Previously he'd lain by Izusa's side as if content to be back home. Now he acted in a restless manner. Izusa stroked his fur and pushed her nose towards his to reassure him.

Later, when the potatoes were ready to be added to beans and dried meat stew, Izusa heard a sound that couldn't be blamed on her cooking chores.

Again Moon got up and paced the floor.

Izusa looked through a small hole in the shutters, which were locked across the windows to keep the weather and strangers out. She could see nothing. Outside, it was the darkest of nights, with the full moon obscured by the thickening snow clouds.

She continued to prepare supper.

She recalled how the journey from Fort St Vrain had been lengthy and now she felt weary. She knew that Mayle Stone would be worried and that he'd berate her for going off on a wild goose chase. He'd look mad enough to swallow a horn-toad backwards. Izusa had smiled as the picture formed in her mind. Then it dissipated as she neared the cabin. Dark and empty.

Moon stopped pacing. He stood as still as a statue. Then his ears pricked up again.

Izusa heard a crunch, crunch, crunch on the outside porch.

Immediately she blew out the candle and sat as still as a statue in the darkness. She signalled to Moon to sit at her side and she stroked his fur. His presence was comforting in the wilderness of the mountains. Izusa put her hands gently on his muzzle and shook her head. Although without speech, the two communicated well.

She tried to make out the sounds. An animal? It wasn't unknown for a wild animal to prowl around. In winter, they had to make sure the horses and mules were safe from predators who were hungry enough to chance their luck and invade human space. She believed it was far too early in the year for wild animals to be desperate enough to come so near. Humans and animals had a healthy respect for each other's dens.

Izusa trembled.

She didn't want to consider the alternative.

Humans.

Maybe it was Stone, she thought, but he would call out and bang the door to be let in. She listened harder. One tap and then another. The sounds stopped at the doorway. Footsteps. The heels of boots. She tried to swallow down her fear. It could be someone seeking shelter, she reasoned, however, she looked around for a weapon and found it clenched in her fist. She held up the small sharp knife she'd used for preparing the meal. A scattergun, which Stone kept ready to fire in case of trouble, lay near the pallet bed but she didn't want to get it and risk making a noise.

Moon lay on the cabin floor. His gaze went from Izusa to the door and back to Izusa. She saw the sparkle of a predator's eyes as the wolf waited for a signal from her.

It was fairly dark in the cabin because as yet, the fire had not started to take hold. Izusa recalled her mother berating her ineptitude with fire skills. Tonight it was to be blessed that she was so awkward. She figured she'd have a fighting chance if she were invisible to a predator.

Rudyman's boots crunched as he attempted to creep across the porch. He hadn't meant to make a noise but wood ash, sprinkled over the wood floor and ground surrounding the cabin, probably in a bid to stop ice coating it, he thought, had caught him out. Stone's horse, he'd tied to a tree by the stables, but away from the cabin for exactly that reason. He shook his squelchy wet boots.

'Could've brought the damn horse to the door,' he moaned. Then he stared at the dark unwelcoming cabin. 'Hope to God this is worth it.'

However, the picture of the woman at the fort came to his mind. When he'd first noticed her near at the fort with the horse and mules, he'd expected to smell the stink of buffalo grease, which he believed Indians used to oil their hair, however, surprisingly, she smelt as earthy as the ground. He recalled her tiny frame and he pictured her trembling inside. He believed that he could almost feel the tension within the cabin walls. He licked his lips, certain he tasted fear, her fear, which floated like motes of dust through the cracks in the woodwork out into the air around him. His nostrils sniffed in the smell of woman.

'I know you're inside.' He hammered on the door. He shouted as the pain from his frozen hands burned him. 'Let me in! Let me in!'

There was no answer and Rudyman kicked at the main door in frustration. Too late, he appreciated it was no way to treat a frozen foot, either. He cried out again. The pain zipped up through his leg, jarred the knee and flew back to a throbbing toe.

The door hadn't moved. It was rigid and solid.

'You blasted squaw,' he shouted. As he hopped around the porch floor, he blamed the pain on the young woman. He screamed with anger when there was no response inside. 'Damn stubbornness. I want you. I'll make you pay for this.'

Cursing, he walked the length of the porch.

'I'll get in – don't you worry.'

His glance took in a door with one tightly shuttered window on either side. It was as if they were designed to give plenty of light into the room when open, he thought, but impenetrable to outsiders when closed. Rudyman stepped off the porch and walked around and his footsteps left a black trail from the ash in the snow. He saw how underneath had been cleverly constructed on natural rocks to raise the floor of the entire log cabin. There were no windows to the back or the sides.

He was struck with an idea as he saw how the lean-to stables were built up against the cabin as if merged into one. He contemplated as he scratched his head. He could see, even in the poor light, that a door in the stable end had been fashioned with extensive hinges to support it. It was so well camouflaged he'd almost missed it.

Standing against the wall was an axe.

He started to grin like a baked possum.

Nimbly, as if well practised, he caught a head louse and squeezed its tiny hard shell between his gloved finger and thumb until it cracked and then he flicked it away.

'Could be a weakness there,' he said. 'That is the way in. I can concentrate on the weak spot.'

He peeped through a knothole in the wood door. He screwed up his one eye as he peered through; with the other, he made out a couple of mules and a cow.

Nothing to concern him, he thought. All they can do is bray and moo.

CHAPTER TEN

Izusa, aware that the hidden door to the stables had been found, sat in the dark and heard the thumps and felt the jolts as the would-be intruder hammered against the woodwork. Mayle Stone had worked as hard as a buster but now the construction looked a bad idea.

A look of desperation crossed her face and her gaze scanned the cabin as she wondered where the best place to hide would be – then it was too late. Rudyman merely pushed opened the door between the stable and the cabin and he was in the room.

Jon Rudyman had forgotten that Izusa also had a wolf as a companion. Before he had time to register the fact, the beast sprang from the floor, its mouth open, as it aimed for Rudyman's neck.

Rudyman instinctively raised his arm. He protected his throat and the beast sank its teeth deeply into his arm instead. He was knocked to the floor by the sheer weight of the animal. They rolled around the floor. As he struggled to get free, he felt for his knife and drew it from his belt. He slashed viciously at the wolf's mouth and snout, wedging it between the animal's teeth until it let go. The wolf snarled as it was forced back but soon readied itself to attack again. Rudyman didn't allow it a second chance; grabbing his gun, he shot as it leapt towards him.

Moon fell to the floor.

Jon Rudyman then turned his attention to the woman.

'I think we've met before,' he said, 'but we didn't introduce ourselves. I'm Jon Rudyman.' Hands on hips, he gave a belly laugh. 'Remember? At Fort Vrain? You didn't think much of me then but now I believe I'll have time to change your mind.'

Izusa turned towards the main door as if she planned to bolt. This brought more laughter. He spluttered and moved his hands to hold his belly as if it hurt him. 'You're not going anywhere and your man is with the ghosts.'

Izusa's eyes opened wide. She frowned in disbelief. A look of horror took its place.

'No. No,' she mouthed.

'Don't be upset. I'm taking his place.' He stepped towards Izusa. 'You could do worse than be with me. I'll keep you warm when it snows outside.'

She backed away from him, glancing left and right as she did.

'Don't try anything,' he warned. Then he laughed again. 'Although I don't think a little thing like you could hurt me.'

He underestimated her.

It was as if at the news of Mayle Stone's death, Izusa became aware that she had nothing left to live for. She'd been pushed out of the Cherokee village and knew they wouldn't have her back, whatever the reason. She glanced towards Moon, her companion, and saw that his white coat was smeared with dark red blood. He lay on the floor. He didn't move.

Her hand tightened around her knife.

The man was twice her size and would probably be able

to deflect any blows she meted out. Momentarily, she shut her eyes and her lips mouthed words.

'You praying?' Rudyman laughed. 'Keep praying, girl. Ain't gonna do you no good.'

Then he saw Izusa ready to attack. The laughter dissolved.

Like the wolf, she threw her body towards him. Too late, he noticed the knife. The knife slashed at his torso and caused him to double up in pain. Izusa wielded the blade expertly as if he was a pig to gut – it pierced his flesh and ripped it to ribbons. Then the blade stuck into his abdomen. She couldn't pull it out so she looked for another weapon. Her hands tore through his cheeks. His face dripped with blood as her nails left a trail. He reeled away from her attack and fell to the floor.

'My god, you're a demon,' he shouted.

Solely his strength and his instinct for survival brought him back to his feet and he charged at her.

Izusa braced herself, ready for the attack then Rudyman's foot caught the wolf's prone body and he flew across the room before hitting the wall behind the bed.

Izusa's face held an expression of incredulity. She hadn't expected to get the upper hand. She stood transfixed at the sight, for a moment, as he started to stir. She looked around wildly for something, anything, to defend herself with; she spied a hammer near the fire.

Rudyman roared and struggled to get up. He looked like a grizzly bear on hands and knees, shaking his body from side to side. She hit him with the hammer – once, twice and then ran.

She didn't have time to grab a coat or boots, she ran quickly across the room. She grabbed a mule. The animal hee-hawed loudly. Then she heard Rudyman's shouts behind her. He grabbed at her clothes. The neck of her doeskin shift pulled tight against her neck and slowed her down. She turned and saw blood running from Rudyman's head. He pulled her body into his and in doing so, pressed the knife, which was still embedded in his body. Cursing, he let her go although not before he punched her and she fell to the floor. He felt for the knife handle and pulled. Blood spurted out and he tried to stem the bleeding.

Izusa crawled away and scuttled under the large bed. She remembered the scattergun and reached for it from under the pallet bed. Then Rudyman was there. He grabbed her foot and pulled her out. She fought against him. The gun fell from her grasp. The fight wasn't one-sided even though Izusa's size was less than half of his. He winced and staggered with the effort of pulling her out. She grabbed the gun again. He pulled at the skirt of her shift. She fired but missed as she fell. The pellets scattered everywhere. He took advantage of her moment of startled disbelief and pulled the gun away from her grasp.

Finally he had the upper hand. She hadn't the strength to continue the battle. He beat her until she collapsed on the floor beside the wolf.

'In different circumstances,' he cursed, 'you and me could've had a good time.'

However, the woman and the wolf had fought a hard battle and he, Rudyman, was wounded. He sat for a while on the edge of the bed.

'I feel so tired,' he said. An inner voice warned him it could be dangerous to stay. Out loud he muttered, 'I've got to get away from here. Big mistake to stay 'cause the woman belonged to the Cherokees and they might seek revenge for killing one of their own.'

The livestock continued to be agitated. The mules kicked their back legs against the stable walls and filled the air with screeching hee-haws. Rudyman put water and coffee on the rekindled fire before he dragged himself through to the stables.

'Shut up, you noisy critters!' The smell of blood seemed to make the animals crazy with fear. 'Shut up, I said.'

Rudyman, quick to avoid the mules' hoofs, grabbed at a spade to paddle them into silence. The mules made even more noise and the cow mooed in unison. Rudyman threw the spade at them before he seemed to understand the futility of his actions.

He moved outside and grabbed at Mayle Stone's horse. It shook its head and backed away but Rudyman pulled sharply at the reins to bring the animal to heel. The horse shook its head from side to side as white frothy saliva thinly streaked with blood poured from its mouth. Although, the horse resisted, it soon became quiet and docile.

Rudyman slapped its neck. 'That's better,' he said.

Then he manoeuvered it indoors and allowed it to drink and feed in the stable while he went back into the house. He gave himself enough time to drink coffee and gnaw at the bits of dried meat. He was acutely aware that wolves moved in packs and he kept glancing through the windows in case there were others out there.

He used the beasts' water to wash the bloodstains from his face and hands. His shirt was torn where the knife had slashed it but to his relief, the wounds weren't as bad as they could have been except where Izusa had plunged the knife in a final frenzy. He tore the sheet from the bed into strips, padded the wounds then used the rest to bind himself together. The damage to his arm was also bad. The wolf's teeth had gouged lumps of flesh out. He poured some of his private stash of whiskey over the wounds, and then packed them with snow to clean and numb the pain before he bound them. He changed into a shirt, which he reckoned had belonged to Mayle Stone and threw his own in a corner.

'Well, he won't need it where he is!' Rudyman grinned.

Less than twenty minutes after drinking the coffee, Rudyman left the log cabin behind. He'd filled his saddle bags from the storeroom to sustain him until he reached a fort or small town.

Izusa and Moon lay together – still and unmoving on the floor.

CHAPTER ELEVEN

Mayle Stone made the journey home.

The mule, left by Jon Rudyman, had no idea which direction it was taking and when he attempted to re-direct it, the beast didn't always choose to pursue Stone's idea of where it ought to go or how fast. It had its own pace to trot. It literally dug its hoofs in. It was also wary of the wolf that trotted at its heels.

Dark Star had returned to wake Stone on the second night when he'd fallen from the mule, exhausted. He'd licked at the man's face until Stone resurfaced into consciousness. Stone used Dark Star's neck fur to pull himself to his feet.

'Don't know what I'd have done without you,' he praised his companion.

Stone shuddered. He did know. He'd have died of exposure out on a night like this. His wounds seemed superficial – it had been the bang to the head that had knocked him out.

'I reckon Jon Rudyman thought I was a goner,' he said. 'All that blood from the wound must've convinced him.'

Now he nestled in a blanket he'd found thrown over the mule.

'Need it more than you,' he said as the mule turned

and stared with a pair of large, almost liquid looking eyes. 'Now I don't believe you're gonna cry. An' if I place my backside on your back – well, it's bound to keep you warm.' The mule turned away as if disgusted. Stone chuckled. 'Come on, Joe,' Stone coaxed. 'Well, I guess I'll call you Joe 'cause I don't know your name.'

The mule's ears pricked up at these words. Stone looked at the crisscross of scars across the mule's back.

'Don't you recognize the tone? Don't worry, old fella, we'll take it at your pace. I think you might respond better that way.'

Stone dozed off a couple of times and, as if it sensed the sleeping man, the mule stopped and grazed on any tufts of grass that peeped through the snow. It was midnight the next day when Stone spied the log mountain cabin.

Moon, no longer white, sat outside and howled. It stopped when it saw his master and Dark Star and then crawled towards them.

Stone halted and stared. He swallowed hard and rubbed his eyes. No smoke came out of the chimney. No woman stood outside chopping logs in the snow. He'd imagined lots of things as he'd wound his way home. The nightmares, both waking and asleep, had jolted him back to reality. He looked over at the log cabin and the nightmare scene continued. Although he'd built the cabin so they could see more than a visitor was able, Izusa wouldn't have had time to douse a fire. Surely Moon would've been inside the cabin with her?

As the wolf came up to him, Stone could see it was covered with blood. It hadn't the energy to bound – it could only stagger and limp towards him.

'Steady, Joe,' he said. The mule baulked at the wolf and tried to run. 'This is our friend, Moon.' He got down and

71

fussed over the wolf that whined at Stone's touch. 'I'll check you over soon, boy. Got to see what's happened to Izusa.'

He walked the mule to the building that served as a stable but as he did this, Moon lay down, head between his paws, and started to growl and howl.

A pain grasped the pit of Mayle Stone's stomach and clutched tightly so he was almost bent double. He took a deep breath.

'What the hell has happened here?' he asked. The mules whinny-brayed and the cow bellowed, its teats full and unmilked, in distress. Now the other wolf's rumbling growl, which came from deep in its chest, added to the crescendo.

It took less than a short burst of time for Stone to appreciate something was very wrong. His addled brain had to process the scene before he turned towards the door that connected the lean-to stable and the cabin and saw it hung from its hinges.

In two strides he was inside the cabin.

'Izusa!' he shouted.

He saw her lifeless form on the floor. He knelt by her side and touched her brow. Immediately she reacted. Her eyes opened wide but they were glazed and unseeing. Automatically her hand moved to his belt and closed around the hilt of his hunting knife and pulled it out. He was unable to stop the knife as she brought it down and towards his chest. Instinct saved his life. He turned and the knife embedded itself deep in his arm instead. He left the knife where it was because he knew he'd have to be ready to stem the flow of blood when he pulled it out.

Izusa fought like a wildcat for a few moments and then she slumped in his grasp, the fight gone. As he held her, he noticed the torn, bloodied shift barely covering her body and blinked back tears of sorrow and anger. He fetched water and a cloth and then removed her ruined clothes and washed her clean. Her face, and body, blackened with bruises and her mouth red from split lips, her hair matted with blood. He picked her up and lay her down on the large bed.

'This bed was going to become our bed. Now a beast has defiled you.'

He covered her frail body with the bearskin and then walked outside. In the empty snowy wilderness, as he pulled the knife from his arm, Mayle Stone howled louder than all the wolves in the pine covered mountains. He placed his hand over the wound but luckily it was superficial. He didn't move for a while but then a plan formed in his mind.

Stone sat for a moment and stroked Moon.

'I bet you were out hunting. Can't feel ill towards you for that. . . . Only, if you'd been in the log cabin then Izusa would've been safe.' His hand came upon something sticky on the wolf's coat and the animal winced. Stone talked soothingly to it and examined the wounds. 'How could I have not noticed?'

The wolf allowed him to touch him without backing away. Stone rubbed snow into its coat to clean it up and to make sure his guess was right.

'You lick the snow, boy, that's the best treatment.'

The wolf's tongue hung from its mouth as it panted in agreement. Then Stone noticed the wolf had a couple of teeth missing and its lower jaw was bloody as well. He nuzzled his head right up to the wolf and put his arms around it.

'Looks as if you did try to defend Izusa's life after all.'

Mayle Stone left water, and a meat and bean stew on a table by the bed. He stood and looked at her for a while. Since he'd washed her, placed her where she was warm and then gone on to fix the door linking the stable, she'd not moved. Her breathing was shallow, almost imperceptible and only when he held a small piece of silvered glass and saw it mist up, was he convinced she was still alive.

Moon sat and looked up at him.

'Keep watch over Izusa,' Stone said. 'I'm going after the man who did this. Don't know what I'll find when I return. Rest will be the best medicine.'

Moon blinked as if he understood Stone's words.

Stone took the scattergun, powder and shots with him as Rudyman had stolen his longrifle.

'I know you've used this scattergun, Izusa, because of all the shots in the wood of the cabin. Have to give you some shooting lessons when I get back. . . .' His voice tailed off.

Moon stayed with Izusa as ordered.

The wolf climbed on to the bed and lay beside her. Its large elongated body stretched out was almost the full length of the woman. At a weight of nearly 150 pounds, it was heavier than Izusa by thirty pounds. Yet the creature was gentle, timid in its manner towards her.

Moon watched the shallow rise and fall of her chest as she slept. The wolf didn't hold the man's fears for her death. It had no cause to think other than the woman was alive but peaceful. He pushed his nose underneath her hand as if giving comfort to her. Her response was weak but she lifted her hand upwards and stroked the fur. The 'cape' hairs on the back were so thick in winter and she nestled her fingers into its coat. Moon was content to lie by her side yet alert, aware of its surrounding, ready to react to everything in perceptible change in the environment.

Over the next few days, Izusa became more conscious, both of her surrounding and of the memories of what had happened. She could smell wolf. It animated a powerful, feral odour of wet dog and wild places. The scent was stronger than usual, muskier, and demonstrated his concern for the woman. Finally she opened her eyes. Moon's long pink tongue licked her face and stared at her out of a pair of yellow gold eyes. She smiled at the faithful animal and went to get up but Moon nudged her and jumped off. She watched as he flicked his tail with its precaudal ring around it – the only natural dark spot on its coat – and gracefully made its way across the room.

Moon lifted a bowl from the side table with his soft mouth and brought it to her bed. Moon nudged her arm as if to encourage her to take the meat broth into her mouth, and then watched as she took a drink of water. Then Moon allowed her to move from the bed and she threw back the bearskin that covered her. Moon howled and moved away from her. She looked down at her naked body and saw what had upset the wolf. Her clenched hands held the side of the bed and she felt she ought to join in with the wolf's howls.

She pulled the sheet she'd lain on, wrapped them all together, and walked towards the door that led out from the log cabin.

CHAPTER TWELVE

After he'd attached a rope halter and thrown a blanket over one of his mules, he backtracked yet again towards the fort. Dark Star trotted at his side. He felt that he couldn't do anything more for Izusa. She'd live or die. Whatever happened, he wanted to kill the varmint who'd caused all this trouble and disrupted their lives. There were no clues around the log cabin; the snow had wiped out the trail. Now the door between the lean-to stable and cabin was mended, it was as if nothing had changed since he'd left to get another sack of flour.

'We're all out, mister,' Bert Wilkins said. 'Thought you were coming two days ago, Tuesday? Anyways, the deal's off – I gave your squaw some flour the other day.'

'Change o' plans,' Stone muttered. He tried hard to focus, his head felt as if it was split in two.

The cause of which, Wilkins observed, was the injury to his head. 'You got a nasty cut there. Best see Doc before yer head falls off.' He sniggered at his own joke.

Stone ignored the man's advice. He told him he'd managed for several days in this condition, a couple more wouldn't hurt him none. Then he got close to the store-keeper. They stood eyeball to eyeball. Wilkins didn't look comfortable about this.

'What's ailing you?' he asked.

'What you mean, Izusa came and got the flour rations?'

'The other day. Only got half a bag, though, that's all I could spare.'

'You know, your left eyeball spins when you're acting shady.'

'OK. I can give you more flour,' he admitted. 'But your sassy little woman, she got the lieutenant to serve her.'

A smile etched itself over Stone's face. 'Well, what d'you know? She ain't such a delicate creature after all.'

'Didn't look at all delicate to me,' Wilkins muttered.

The remark jolted Stone back to the present. 'I'm looking for information,' he said. 'A critter, Jon Rudyman, he was here the same time as me an' I guided him to Deadman's Plate, but we split up. I need to find him. We got unfinished business.' Stone grimaced and his hand touched his jaw.

'It broken?' he asked.

Stone shook his head. 'I came to see if he'd returned here.'

'You and some other people want to speak to Rudyman. The army commander is asking questions about that old man, Lee Bandy. Everyone thought he'd died from a dicky heart. I mean, he was seventy if he was a day. However, it turns out that someone had parted the hair on his head with the butt of a gun.' Wilkins stared at Stone's head. 'Bit like yours,' he commented.

Stone made his way over to the largest building in the fort where he knew he'd most likely find the commander. The fort only held a small showing of military although it was rumoured the commander kept asking for more men. According to him, as the eastern settlers advanced west, Indian attacks were becoming common. Stone looked at the name on the door, Second Lieutenant George Casey Peterson.

'You stay here, Dark Star, don't want our Second Lieutenant to think I'm intimidating him,' Stone said.

Dark Star waited outside as ordered yet Stone knew he only had to whistle and 200 pounds of a slavering beast would be at his side. He knocked but didn't wait to be invited in. It was warmer in Peterson's office than outside. The place was full of soldiers. Stone walked towards the log fire and warmed his backside.

'Can I help you?'

Stone counted the stripes on the man's arm to make sure he spoke to the main man. He moved across to the desk.

'Yes, Lieutenant Peterson? I'm Mayle Stone.'

He purposely gave him a higher ranking as he held out his hand. In Stone's experience, a genuine confident man would compliment him for the honour but nevertheless correct him. The soldier shook Stone's hand but made a show of brushing his hand on his pants afterwards. Stone said nothing although he pushed away the unsettling feeling that Peterson was going through the motions of politeness. He didn't ask his visitor to sit down and they stood facing each other across the desk. The other soldiers had dispersed into the background. Then Peterson looked up to Stone, blinked hard and stared at him. He had to lift his chin to equalize Stone's height.

'Your name's Mayle Stone? You're the man who's a friend of this Jon Rudyman?'

Stone turned his head away and spat on the floor. 'He's no friend of mine, just the opposite. The man tricked me and made a beeline for my home, and . . .' He paused for a moment then added, 'And my woman.'

The lieutenant's mouth opened and his tongue flapped

as he tried to recover from the shock. 'Your wife?'

'Yes, my woman, Izusa of the Cherokees.'

'A squaw?'

'My Cherokee woman.'

'But a squaw, thank goodness. For a moment I thought she was a respectable woman.'

Mayle Stone grabbed the lapels of the Second Lieutenant and lifted him to the same height so he didn't have to raise his eyes to see him properly.

'I don't see what difference that should make to you, Second Lieutenant Peterson. And here I was, going to thank you for helping her get served in the store.'

'That's your er . . . er . . . woman?' Peterson struggled to get the words out.

'Yes.'

'Oh yes, I recall. She asked, or rather she drew your name in the flour – wanted to know where you were. Well, she's gone from here now. Got her flour and I told her to go home.'

'She went home. Someone else was there and attacked her. She's near to death now. I think I know who it was. I want to find him. Can you spare anyone to help?'

'I have very few men,' Peterson choked out. 'I have to investigate a murder here.'

Stone let the man drop back on to his feet. The lieutenant swayed but put his hand out to prevent his shaking legs from giving way.

'I don't like the way you are acting, Mr Stone.' Now, literally on firmer ground, Peterson's arrogance returned. 'However, we are possibly looking for the same man so perhaps we ought to help each other. Of course, you can't argue that a man's murder is more important than, er, an incident involving a sq— I mean, your woman. I mean, aren't they meant to be, er . . . accommodating? So it doesn't affect them in the same way as our white women.'

Mayle Stone drew back his arm while bunching his fist. He delivered the package to the lieutenant. The last words the soldier heard, if he heard anything, was from Stone.

'The incident with the "er ... squaw ... er ... woman" is the only thing that matters to me.'

Unfortunately for Stone, the other soldiers in the room reappeared from the shadows. They'd witnessed the incident. They'd witnessed everything but evidently decided this was a step too far when they saw the Second Lieutenant as he flew backwards from the force of the blow from Mayle Stone's fist. A soldier pushed his gun into Stone's back and ordered him to the gaol house. Stone had no choice. It was prison or a bullet. He held up his hands as ordered and walked out as instructed.

'Keep that wolf under control,' the soldier ordered. 'Or it'll take a bullet as well.'

'Stay,' Stone said. 'Wait for me.'

Dark Star lay down with his head on paws; its green sparkling gaze followed every move the soldier and Stone made.

'So this Jon Rudyman has caused trouble here?' Stone asked. The soldier prodded the gun into his back. 'It's only a question,' Stone protested but didn't turn or slow his pace to antagonize the man.

'The lieutenant thinks he might have something to do with Bandy's death. And it seems there's a couple of wanted dodgers around that look like him. Not the same name ... seems he changes that in every town he visits.'

'Serious then?'

'Murder, robbery, assault, you name it, he's done it.'

'How come nobody's caught up with him?'

'He don't stay long in one place or another. Only got

this information 'cause a bounty hunter has been trailing him. Mighty put out he missed him again. He's still around so I think he'll want to speak to you if you know anything about Rudyman.'

They reached the place that served as a gaol in the far right corner of the fort. As they'd walked and talked, the soldier's gun had become less painful in Stone's back. He'd relaxed in Stone's company which turned out unfortunate for the soldier because when Stone was about to enter the gaol, he swung round. He knocked the rifle from the soldier's grip and followed it up with a blow to the chin. Completely unprepared, the soldier made no attempt to put up a defence. The man fell to the ground like a sack of stones.

Mayle Stone took the keys from the soldier's belt, pushed the door a bit wider and dragged him into the back of the cell. Conveniently, two sets of chains were set in the floor to hook any prisoner. Stone clamped them around both hands and feet of the soldier then tied the man's neckerchief over his mouth to stop him shouting for help.

'Sorry about this but I don't have time to hang around here. Got some man hunting to do.' He locked the cell door and threw the keys outside – out of the soldier's view. 'They'll have to get a blacksmith to unlock you. Unless they've got a spare set.' He also left the soldier's gun outside. 'I'm tempted to take this but don't want to be accused of stealing military property.'

Stone stealthily retraced his steps back to the store where he'd left his mule. He didn't have to whistle for Dark Star – as he stepped out of the gaol, the wolf came immediately to his side.

As he unhitched the mule, he reflected that he was nowhere nearer to finding Jon Rudyman than he had been when he'd arrived here. He screwed up his face in irritation, as if he'd been wrong not to trail him from the cabin rather than try to second-guess that he'd made his way back to the fort. He could be miles away now. He mounted his mule and started to make his way out. He hadn't got very far when another rider caught him up.

'You Mayle Stone?'

Automatically Stone's hand touched his knife at his waist. He wished he had taken the handgun. No time to fire a scattergun.

'Don't know him.'

'Well, the description from Lieutenant Peterson fits you. Although, now he's regained consciousness, he's under the impression that you're being held as a guest in his cells.'

Stone made no comment but the man continued as if it made no difference to him anyway.

'I hear we got a mutual friend.' The man touched his hat and introduced himself. 'I'm Ray Heston. Bounty hunter. This is the tool of my trade.' He tapped the short barrel shotgun in his saddle holster. 'I hear you met up with someone I'm after, Jon Rudyman. At least that's the name you know him as, I believe.'

Stone held his peace as if he wasn't willing to share any information with a bounty hunter. His lips set in a hard line. He wanted Jon Rudyman for himself. To kill.

Heston continued, 'There's ten thousand dollars on his head. I'm willing to give you a cut.'

'Don't want any money.'

Heston pushed his hat up and down his forehead as if stirring up his brains. 'Well, doesn't that take it all? How's about I give you a hundred dollars if you tell me where you last seen him? An' then I won't tell our friend Peterson you just broke outta his gaol.'

Stone was about to steer his mule away but he didn't want to cause a fracas and he certainly didn't want to risk being hauled back to the fort.

'Don't want any money. The other fella offered me a share in his mine. I refused that as well. I've got all that I need,' Stone explained. 'I did guide Rudyman to Deadman's Plate. Seems he's got a map of a mine at Yellow Rock Creek.'

Heston pulled his hat back on his head. 'I thankee kindly, sir,' he responded. 'If I catch him, I'll leave you some money at the fort anyways for the information. Perhaps you'll be able to bribe Peterson with it. He's gonna be mighty sore about you escaping.'

Heston clicked his teeth, hauled on the horse's reins to get the horse to move. He made his way back to the valley. Only Jon Rudyman concerned him now.

In the distance, Stone turned and glimpsed the figure ride through the thickening snow. It was the second time he'd watched a man ride on into the valley.

He hoped Ray Heston would be OK but then Stone guessed the man knew how to survive. Then he put his head down and rode in the opposite direction.

CHAPTER THIRTEEN

Mayle Stone headed back towards home, no nearer in his quest than when he left. All he'd managed to do was cause trouble with the US cavalry. Then a wry smile crossed his face as he reflected that the probability was by the time he returned to the fort, the lieutenant would've moved on. He was someone who didn't want to stay in a small posting or he'd make such a mess of the situation he'd be sent to another post. Stone's mouth turned down at the corners. No, it would be his luck that the lieutenant would prefer to fight Indians, protect 'decent folk' and wait for him to return to the fort for retribution.

In the log cabin everything was as he left it. Almost.

Izusa no longer lay on the bed. Moon hadn't come to greet him. The water and food were barely touched. The sheet and the bearskin had gone. Dark Star looked up at his master and waited. Stone patted the wolf's head.

'We'll find her.'

Yet what could he do? Going to the fort had proved useless and the falling snow left it impossible to track him. Now Izusa was gone without a trace. They'd lived together for over two years and her absence would leave a big gap in his life.

Then it dawned on him that she could've moved to the

smaller of the cabins. He'd built it for her. It was almost a place of refuge. The thought gave him a surge of energy and he headed up the hill.

'Izusa!' He called her name several times as he walked towards the cabin. 'Moon!'

There was no reply. He opened the door, still hoping to the last moment that she'd be on the bed, asleep with Moon.

The place was cold and empty. He returned to the larger cabin and slumped down on the bed. He had no plan in mind. He looked around the room, saw the neatly woven decorations Izusa had placed around the room. At the head of the bed she'd placed a dream catcher to fight off the demons of nightmares.

Then he noticed a torn, bloodied shirt in the corner of the room. It brought him from his reminiscing – all that remained now was the dream of someone he'd grown to love – and back to reality. He picked up the shirt. Dark Star snarled. Stone allowed the wolf to sniff and worry the material.

'Come on, Star, we got to go and find him.'

A picture of Izusa again crossed his mind but he shook it away. He couldn't remain strong if she cluttered his thoughts. Even if she wasn't dead, it was clear to him that she didn't want to be found. Otherwise why would she leave the cabin?

Stone changed mules and took a fresh one on the journey to find Rudyman. He took the other man's mule with him. He determined to exchange it for his own horse. He checked his gunpowder was dry and he had plenty of shots and his hunting knife was secured in his belt. Dark Star sniffed and ran all around the outside of the log cabin and stables before it gave an excited yap and started to turn in circles.

'Follow!' Stone commanded.

Dark Star had his nose stuck determinedly to the ground. Although it was still snowing, it seemed it hadn't washed the other man's stink away. He knew he'd have to take shelter before nightfall. He could carry on but common sense told him to rest up, keep warm and take in food.

'No good being half dead when I come across the critter,' Stone muttered.

Later he found a crevice in the rocks. It was too small for a large animal to hibernate, but big enough to give some shelter to a human being, and a wolf. The two mules huddled against the wall to shelter from the wind. He wore an oilskin duster that provided him with a tent-like structure to keep him dry. He made coffee and spitted two rabbits he'd killed earlier over a small fire he fashioned from twigs, bark and a couple of small branches, to provide food for a couple of meals. He threw another to Dark Star, who didn't seem too particular about having it roasted and it was gone before Stone took a few bites of his meal. Finally he leaned his back against the dry wall and closed his eyes.

It was only evident that a new day had dawned from the lighter sky glimpsed through snow clouds. It had stopped snowing but Stone, from experience, guessed it was temporary. He had a drink of water, ate the rest of the rabbit before throwing Dark Star the bones. The mules drank the rest of the melted snow and ate some grains. He held out the shirt.

'Here, Star,' he said.

Dark Star barked.

They were on the trail again.

Stone, his mules and his wolf plodded on. It was as if they were all so focused on their quarry nothing detracted

86

them from their goal. Not the cold, nor the wind or the increasing snow which spun around and enveloped them all and gradually slowed them down.

Dark Star went in front of Stone and his mules. Sometimes his snout pushed into the snowy ground and sniffed and barked before it ran on again. Stone was sure the animal was still on track and he followed him without question. At this moment the wolf was his only hope.

The wind tore at his beaver skin hat and the snow tried to creep underneath it but it was secured with a scarf. His beard growth – the only time he revealed his face was in spring and summer – kept his chin warm.

He kept up the relentless pace – moving from mule to mule to give them a rest – while he followed the wolf. Even the wind-broken mule sensed his determined spirit and kept pace. It was far into the night again when Stone came to a halt. It was another natural break in the rocky landscape and he needed to rest up again. He was barely able to stand as he hitched and unsaddled the mules. He needed food and drink before he did anything else.

'No point in catching up with Rudyman if I've got no strength to fight,' he said.

He cleared a piece of ground so the mules had grass and then he ate some of the rabbit he'd cooked the previous night while he set a can of coffee to brew. He threw the rabbit bones to the ground when he'd finished. Dark Star mopped up the leftovers and waited for more.

'Got a bit of dried jerky.' Stone laughed. 'Can't do better than that yet.'

He had no plan to confront Rudyman. He wanted to sneak up on him and then get the gist of the situation. He hadn't thought any further than that with regards to his foe. He wanted to surprise him but then, apart from maybe skinning or roasting him alive, he didn't know what tack his revenge would take.

Stone also thought about Ray Heston the bounty hunter and wondered where he was now. He'd gone off in the direction of Deadman's Plate but he didn't know whether he'd given up and turned back to the fort or continued to look for clues.

He recalled the hard look in the bounty hunter's eyes that said that no one could have Rudyman until he had finished with him. Stone hoped to prove him wrong. At last, tuckered out, he fell into a deep sleep. He was woken a few hours later by Dark Star nuzzling his nose into his face. The animal whined, barked and scratched the ground until Stone sat up and took notice.

'You found something, Star?'

The wolf barked as if in answer. It was tempting to rush off. The wolf, Stone judged, had come across Jon Rudyman's trail again. Nothing else would excite it so much as to have found the owner of the scent they were tracking. Stone threw the wolf another bit of dried meat as a thank you and then made sure the traces of fire were covered with snow.

'For all I know,' he said to his wolf, 'someone could be tracking me!'

When Stone came across a camp several miles on, it was plain that he'd shortened the distance between them. The fire, which Rudyman hadn't bothered to cover, still had some warmth. Stone remounted and kept riding onwards. He kept Dark Star near him. He didn't want Rudyman to be alerted to their presence too soon.

CHAPTER FOURTEEN

Jon Rudyman rode towards the next state.

He took a route that would take him through Devil's Gulch. It would shorten the journey and get him out of Colorado. His mind reeled with the things that had happened in such a short space of time. He felt he'd outstayed his welcome in the Rockies. Utah seemed a good bet. Out of this snow and into the desert maybe? He also considered whether it was time for another change of name. Yet who'd connect him with the death of an old codger or the huntsman and his squaw?

'No one will look for those two, I figure, either now or in the spring. They're unlikely to be missed and the wolves, coyotes and vultures would pick their bones clean.' He looked around him as if his words had conjured up a picture. 'Damn wolves,' he muttered.

His left arm had swollen with the injuries inflicted by those yellow fangs and the ripped flesh pressed against the fabric of his cotton shirt. He wriggled his arm as he tried to get comfortable but then cried out in pain. He cursed the wolf loudly and his voice echoed around the canyon as it bounced from rock to rock. Before dark descended, he looked for a suitable place to stay for the night. He turned and watched the snow cover his tracks. It was as if no one had ever passed this way.

At times, Rudyman wished he'd taken a mule from the stables and reckoned even the broken-winded beast he'd left behind would've made better time than the horse. The mule would've been surer footed on its broader hoofs. The horse's ears pricked up and it neighed loudly. Rudyman paused and looked round at the plain white scene around him.

'Ain't nothing there, you stupid horse.'

Nevertheless, he shivered and pushed his boots into the horse's sides to move on, careful not to injure it with his spurs. A man without a horse was as good as dead.

His eyes felt heavy and the horse was slowing down. Occasionally his eyes closed and then he'd wake up with a start and look around. He shivered. He rode for a day and night and slept fitfully in his saddle. At last he found a suitable spot and drew to a halt and almost fell, exhausted, from his saddle. He gave the horse a loose rein after he'd unsaddled it to allow it to forage for food.

Then he lit a fire for warmth and to brew coffee.

Later, both man and beast huddled near the campfire. The horse stayed within the circle of warmth but kept a good distance away from the man. Rudyman used a canvas sheet propped up with two sticks to keep the wind from him. It didn't work too well and every so often he was forced to chase it down as a gust of wind whipped under the canvas and yanked it up.

The weather was miserable, worse than he'd anticipated for this time of the year, and he wasn't properly prepared to travel, it seemed. The holes in his boots sucked up the snow and turned to water inside which coated his socks with ice. He'd meant to get an oilskin slicker because the ankle length wool coat was threadbare and now, like his socks, wet and heavy. He tugged at his coat sleeve but it seemed as if his arm was fixed. He looked at the swollen appendage.

'Got to get me to a sawbones. This ol' thing is gonna go bad,' Rudyman moaned.

If that wasn't sufficient, Rudyman's journey became even more unpleasant.

'What the hell's that?' He attempted to tune into all the noises he heard and cupped his ear. 'A wolf howling, a girl crying?' He jumped as if to avoid something. 'Is that a bullet?' Rudyman wiped his brow now swathed in sweat with his arm and winced with pain as he did so. Then he stood up. 'Is that the sound of that old broken-winded mule? No.' He shook his head from side to side. 'That raspy breath ol' beast couldn't have followed me.'

Then just as he sat down, the canvas sheet flapped hard again but this time fell over the campfire, reducing it to a pile of embers. The coffee spilt, wet his pants, and hissed across the hot stones. Even though he tried to catch it, the fire was doused completely.

'Damn tarnation!'

He cursed loudly. He cursed the old man, the fur trapper, the woman and the wolf. He blamed everyone for his problems except himself. It seemed as if he didn't want to acknowledge that if he'd left the fort straight away as planned and headed for the next state, he would be there now.

'Not in this hell o' a place. "Lust will get the better of you, boy, knock yer senses awry," my pa used to say.' He spoke to no one anyone else could see. 'Yeah. I know I'd be safe in the warmth of a saloon, with food and drink, and a woman in my arms.'

He pulled the canvas from the flames and shook off the

ashes. He didn't bother to make another fire.

'I don't intend to stay around here past dawn,' he muttered.

Stone finally caught up with Rudyman, yet he didn't immediately confront him. He thought he'd settle down and think things through. It didn't take him more than fifteen minutes to make camp. He swept the snow away with his hands from a small area to avoid the fire dropping down through melted snow.

'Thank goodness it's not too deep,' he said.

Afterwards, he scraped off slivers of birch bark and pulled lichen that hung like old men's beards from the branches to use as kindling. He found plenty of tinder using the dead branches from the bottom of nearby spruces and soon gathered enough bits of wood to keep the fire going overnight. He used his knife, striking it with a piece of sharp quartz to produce a spark, and blew softly until the bark and lichen caught the flames. Unlike Rudyman, he didn't think it a sensible idea to go without a fire, even for a few hours.

After he'd supped, he sought out and then watched the antics of Jon Rudyman. He marked his way with flaming resin-seeped pine knots, a method he often used to find his way back to camp when he'd gone hunting.

Dark Star followed, belly almost to the ground, and then lay by his side while Stone watched Rudyman. His upper lip shivered and his gaze moved from Stone to Rudyman but kept quiet as instructed.

Occasionally his tongue lapped across his lips as if tasting blood on them.

As the night turned from bad to worse for Rudyman, Stone smiled and watched. He had a rule, only to kill what he needed, never for sport. This time he would break the rules. He decided he'd play games with his quarry first. Normally he tracked his prey and made a quick clean kill. Now he was a cat tormenting a rat.

Stone had a whole range of calls he used to trap beasts. He had calls for challenging, mating, noises for beasts in distress, and a whole range of noises that would draw them towards him, some out of sheer curiosity. When he hunted, he'd take out the oldest, or the injured. That way, he reasoned, he wouldn't weaken a pack or herd.

He grinned as he stared at Rudyman who was almost crying over the coffee he'd spilt over his pants.

'I reckon I'll be doing the world a favour, taking you out.'

Rudyman pulled the canvas closer. He scanned his camp-site as if sure he'd heard something nipping around the outskirts. He picked up his rifle.

'I'm ready for you . . . whatever you are. You think you sound like a lion? Well, I eat big cats for breakfast.' He laughed. It was high. Unnatural. 'I know you're every-where in this part of the country. Can't fool me by turning white in winter. I can see your footprints.' He fired. 'Got you.'

Snow cascaded down and exposed only bare rock. The sound of the gunshot stopped as the silent snow sucked it up. For a while it stayed silent and still. Then several minutes later, the growl of a bear rolled across towards him. Rudyman fired his rifle again. The shot went up in the air. Into the rocks and the pine trees. Nothing else.

'I gotta light me a fire. Keep those creatures away.'

Frantically, he stumbled across the ground towards the now extinct fire. He lost his balance as his cold feet skidded across a patch of ice. He cried out with pain as his body slammed against the ground. He lay still, momentarily stunned by the impact of body against hard snow, then rolled over and crawled to the old fire.

He sparked the stones together but the damp wood and the wet kindling refused to fire up. He lay, head down, until Rudyman could see no option but to leave camp. He looked towards where he tied his horse.

It was gone.

Rudyman scrambled to his feet and looked around.

'This place gives me the ejits,' he said. 'It's haunted. The horse had the sense to run. Yet I'm dang sure I tied it. I ought to have hobbled it.'

He blubbered with fear.

'Nothing has gone right since I saw that trapper and Indian at the fort.' He walked around in circles as if driven mad by it all. 'It's her fault. I was smitten by her weird beauty. Everything I did would have had another woman begging for mercy and yet she'd not made a sound. Bitch! Tried to spoil my pleasure. I like a bit of reaction. I like to watch a woman struggle and cry and scream for mercy.'

His hand went to his face where she'd scratched him.

'Although she didn't entirely play dead,' he chortled. 'Now where the hell did that damn horse go?'

Stone listened to Rudyman.

He listened to Rudyman's ramblings about Izusa and his grip on Dark Star's coat tightened. The wolf looked towards Stone and went to rise, eager to make a move.

'No. We'll wait a bit longer,' Stone whispered. 'I'll know when the time is right.' His face screwed up and his expression showed hate amongst a multitude of other emotions.

The wind howled and snowflakes whirled about like mini tornadoes.

Rudyman now sat with his back against a rock and pulled the canvas tightly over his body. He rubbed his hands together to bring heat to them but they were numb. He'd heard of men losing their fingers, toes, and even their nose as the cold turned them black and useless. He tried, initially, to find his horse but it became easier to sit and allow his eyelids to close. But it was only for a split second. The howl of a wolf, which sounded so near, made his eyes open so wide they bulged from their sockets. He sat up straight and looked around, picked up his gun, but almost dropped it as his grip failed him. He grimaced with pain as he forced his fingers around the gun.

'Who is there?' he shouted.

Rudyman jumped to his feet. Yet nothing appeared out of the darkness. His tiredness and apathy had gone.

'Come out and fight,' he screeched. 'I don't want to be chased by nameless demons.'

Another noise caught his attention.

'Is that a mule?'

He walked towards the sound. He stopped and the hair on the back of his neck stood up and a shudder racked him as if someone had walked over his grave.

'Is that the goddamn mule I left in Stone's stables?'

A violent sickness enveloped him and forced his body to bend over. He retched until only watery bile trickled from his mouth.

'It's in exactly the same spot I left the horse.'

He scanned the area about him. The look on his face said he didn't know whether it was God or the devil who'd left the present. The mule kicked its back legs as Rudyman approached him. Rudyman stayed his hand. In different circumstances, he would've taken a stick to the creature. Now soft words came out naturally. Both looked surprised by the sound. Neither man nor beast had heard platitudes uttered from Rudyman's lips before. Rudyman touched it to make sure it wasn't a dream and then, reassured, he moved around the campsite and picked up anything that would be useful.

'Perhaps things will turn out OK. What you think, you broken-winded mule?' he said, as he secured his pack to the animal.

CHAPTER FIFTEEN

Izusa buried the cloth she'd lain on. It was as if by doing so, she'd cleanse her body from the touch of the man who'd attacked her.

She wrapped the bearskin around her and walked and walked. Moon looked up at her, a querulous frown seemed to cover his face but nevertheless he followed her without a command. Her bare feet, seemingly unaffected by the snow covered ground, showed no ill effects from the cold.

A couple of times, Izusa fell and curled up and slept where she lay. Each time Moon dragged the bearskin over her and then nestled up by her side.

Finally, Moon decided it was time to leave Izusa.

The wolf, lean, long and light, loped slowly into the Cherokee camp.

Its small ears sat erect on its large head and they twitched at any sound and the amber gold eyes looked intensely around. Its paws left prints a man could place his foot inside. A few children hid behind the adults as the wolf's mouth drew back to expose large teeth set in black gums. A couple of teeth were missing but it had enough left to cause a lot of damage. No one challenged the beast. The Cherokees knew of the wolf. Its unusually pure white fur had boosted the wolf's almost magical status within the Cherokee people.

Moon knew his way instinctively as if he followed Izusa's family smell. He moved through the wary crowds and stopped at the hut that housed the Chief.

It stood outside and waited.

Word had been brought to Sharka's mate, Big Heart, immediately, that the animal had approached the camp. Now he came out of his dwellings and looked at Moon. Then he frowned. He bent down and touched the dark marks on its chest.

'Blood,' Big Heart said.

He With A Wolfskin, formerly Lightfoot, stepped forward. Moon snarled at the man who wore its mother's coat.

'Look, its mouth is clean. He has not caused the bloodshed. Neither is the animal hurt. It must be his master, Grizzly Bear, or. . . .' He hesitated. 'Or Izusa.'

'I'll send the medicine woman,' Big Heart said. 'And you, He With A Wolfskin, go with her. Your help might be needed.'

The two followed the wolf. The old woman, known as Noname, and not as fast as the young brave, still managed to keep up. She used his footsteps to hasten her way through the snow. Neither spoke but their faces showed concern. Mayle Stone had never asked for help. He'd lived quietly in the woods and, like them, was akin with nature. He hunted with crafted tools and bartered with the white man or the Indians for anything else he needed.

He With A Wolfskin knew Stone treated Izusa kindly. It had been a good trade off for the girl who was a half-sister but blighted by a white skin. No brave would've paired with her because of this deformity, indeed her mother had been treated with derision by the other women because she'd kept the baby and not allowed the gods to decide its fate. In the end it'd been a good choice. He had gained a magnificent wolfskin even though his arrow hadn't killed it. The fact that he'd taken a wolfskin from a white man, even one with a trace of Cherokee blood, had given him kudos and a rise in status.

They journeyed over halfway to Mayle Stone's cabin when they came across a bearskin almost covered with snow.

'Izusa!'

The medicine woman checked the young woman's pulse. She nodded.

He With A Wolfskin waited for a moment to be reassured that the medicine woman had no problems for him to deal with and then left to check the cabin.

Without the burden of the old woman, he stepped up his pace and reached the cabin within the hour. Everything was dark, cold and still. The hair at the back of his neck prickled and he sensed that something evil had happened. He thought it was an odd place with its two beds. Why two? The ashes of the fire still held some warmth in the depths of the hearth. The food, dried in the pots, smelt as if it had only been left for a short while. There was no sign of Mayle Stone. The young brave frowned. He knew the Colorado Mountains to be an inhospitable place.

'If that Grizzly Bear is out there, he won't survive.'

Noname pulled the covers from the girl's face.

'I will heal you, broken one.'

Tears welled in Izusa's eyes but she kept them tightly shut as if she didn't want to be part of this world.

'I'll take you home and you'll get better again.' The medicine woman shushed reassuringly at the young woman. 'You'll become whole,' she said.

Again Izusa entered the village of her people.

Everyone stopped, transfixed by the sight. Then someone ran to fetch Sharka.

'Sharka! Sharka!'

A woman looked up from the fire. She frowned. Didn't they know she had to baste the meat?

'It's Izusa.'

'Izusa?' The name came out breathlessly from her lips. 'What do you mean?'

'She has returned.'

Sharka closed her eyes as if it was a bad dream. When she opened them, the messenger still stood there. They repeated the news.

'No. She can't come back here,' Sharka replied.

Although Big Heart had given her shelter and succour and Sharka was grateful for his generosity, she believed Izusa's return might stretch his magnanimity too far.

Sharka's mind went back to a time which, to her, seemed as if it were only yesterday. . .

'There's a monster down by the river!'

Sharka glanced up from stripping the antelope skin and looked round for her daughter. She had disappeared.

Sharka flew down towards the river as if her feet had wings. She ignored the pounding of her heart that beat against her ribs almost as loud as a warrior's drum.

'Izzy, Izzy, where are you?' The words came as grunts, her lungs hadn't enough air in them to run and shout, but, she thought, it was just as well. She didn't want to bring attention to her daughter. Almost at the river she slowed, her frantic glance took in the *mise en scène*, as frantically she searched for the monster, too.

There it was – rising from the water in a pale haze. Its skin and hair, pure white, and its eyes glinted like glass.

'Mama,' it mouthed although no word came – just a soft grunt.

Sharka scooped up the dripping wet child and rushed away into the woods.

Her partner, Big Heart, heard about the incident. 'I thought I told you to keep that child away from sight. Our people won't tolerate her being around them. She'll bring them bad luck.'

Sharka's eyes shut against his rage. It didn't, however, stop the words from her ears. He squatted close and his anger, although spoken in whispers, to Sharka, was as loud as thunder.

'I was wrong to let you keep it.' Sharka shuddered every time he referred to the child as 'it'. 'You ought to have killed it as it left your womb. Or I ought to have made you leave it behind when I found you.'

The words were empty threats. He hadn't known the extent of the child's defects until later. It was wrapped and swaddled and he'd not been interested in a girl.

It was times like this that she wished she hadn't fallen in love with the little mite. The baby had smiled the first time she'd been put to breast. How could she not have loved it?

It was many months later when Sharka had watched her yawn she knew she'd made the biggest mistake of her life.

'Are you listening?' He continued his rant. 'You have to get rid of it now.'

Sharka's eyes were round as she mirrored his horror. 'No!'

The man looked surprised at the reaction. She was his woman, not a warrior. 'It was all right when you kept her

101

with you but now her ugliness has been revealed,' he said.

She touched his arm. Her fingers delicately danced across his skin.

'Please,' she reasoned. 'One more chance.' He said nothing so she continued. 'I will make sure she understands her position in this household. She will not look at you or at anyone else.' She smiled. 'And I've kept my promise to produce strong sons. We have two already.'

Fortunately, he didn't divorce her – as always, he left his things in their home.

After the lakeside dip, Izusa found her place in the world. She learned that she was a monster. Although Sharka promised her she was loved, Izusa knew that another attempt at freedom meant exile at best, at worst, death.

She prayed daily to the spirits to allow things to return to its natural order and find a place in the world for her daughter. She was presented with an answer when her son returned to camp with a magnificent wolfskin. The animal had been killed by another but offered in compensation for the loss of an antelope kill.

'And the hunter?' Sharka asked. 'He lives alone?'

'He is the man we know as Grizzly Bear. He is the one who saved you and Izusa.'

Now her daughter was back.

'What has she done? Was he repulsed by her?' And yet, Sharka reasoned, 'He let her stay for more than two years. Bring her to me.'

'She is with the Medicine Woman, Noname.'

Izusa lay in the bed and Sharka and Noname tended to her. They made her drink some tea seeped from the roots of the blackberry plant as Izusa constantly held her stomach, indicating pain. Gently, Sharka pressed her daughter's abdomen.

The medicine woman said, 'No. There is no child.'

'Perhaps she can't have any and that's why she's been turned away?' Sharka wiped away her tears. Of course the girl was barren. It was only another affliction to add to the many others, she thought.

The decoction would also soothe her swollen tissues and joints and be a tonic for the whole of her system.

They used salve made from Greenbriar to soothe the cuts and grazes on Izusa's body. They also used Mullein roots in a warm concoction to reduce the swelling in her daughter's feet.

Izusa held her mother's hand, then touched her stomach again and pointed to the Saloli gatoga plant that the medicine woman had hung up to dry earlier that day.

Sharka stared, surprised at her daughter's request.

'The bleeding will stop naturally,' Noname said. 'It is your moon time.' Izusa's mouth shaped into an O. Her face pictured her surprise.

'Has it never happened before?'

Izusa lowered her eyelids, and kept them closed for a while, as if the idea was too much to consider.

CHAPTER SIXTEEN

Although he kept a good distance behind, Stone didn't let his prey out of his sight for a moment.

'It's like we're tracking game, Dark Star,' Stone said. 'That man on the mule.'

The wolf moved ahead to close the gap between the two riders but Stone whistled softly and brought him back.

'You'll get your chance to play,' he added. 'And from how these tracks are panning out, I credit the man's a bigger idiot than I thought – he's on the right path for Devil's Gulch.'

Ahead, Rudyman tried to shake away the feeling he was being followed.

He thought he'd seen a wolf. A black hell-wolf running behind him, then to the side and right when he thought it would attack, it disappeared. He blinked his eyes rapidly as he tried to expel the vision. It was such a quick glimpse that he decided it must've been an overactive imagination. He confided in the mule that folk got fanciful thoughts when they were out in the wilderness.

'Happened to me once when I strayed off the trail in the desert. I'd been sure there was a whole lake of water ahead of me.' He continued to tell the story, unaware that the mule didn't understand. 'I was lucky to find the path again and find real water – at least enough water to shake the damn lake from my mind. By the time I'd got outta that patch of desert, I knew the names of every damn last lizard. Why, we had conversations that lasted for days!'

The snow increased, but it hadn't covered everything.

'Maybe that wolf could've been a half submerged rock.'

He grinned at the thought but his face hurt. His scarf had slipped and snow clung to his beard, lips and cheeks, like icicles. He couldn't feel the tip of his nose but it was still there as it hurt when he attempted to brush the snow away. At least his hands were covered again. He'd found his gloves and although the leather had been soaking wet, and he'd screamed with pain when he pulled them on, they provided more protection than nothing. He looked down and saw they were coated with ice.

'I won't try to take them off until we get to a homestead or fort. They look as if they're a second skin now.' He talked to the mule like a friend. 'You know, beast, I was damn sure I'd left you back at that stable. I must have got mixed up but I sure believe you're better than any horse.' The mule twitched its ears and snorted.

Rudyman rode all day. He frowned. 'Sure thought I'd make it to some sort of shelter by now.' He looked up at the sky. 'Can't tell whether it's day or night. I know I have to stop.'

Finally, he found a place he could shelter. A cave. He directed the mule into the mouth of the cave and then collected as much kindle as he could from the ground inside. He told the mule all about his fears but the mule merely stared with its ears laid back and didn't reply.

'Don't want to risk going deeper into it,' he said. 'It would be just my luck to find a snoozing grizzly bear.'

Rudyman found it difficult to rub the flint to create a

spark over the kindling. His gloved hands hurt and blood welled at the wrists and little globules dropped on to the ground. He didn't seem to notice the blood as finally a spark flashed and he got on his knees and covered the kindling and softly blew the spark to flames. His face warmed against the heat of the fire and he smiled.

As if in sync, Mayle Stone chose a spot in which to settle down. Likewise, he made a fire. Only difference was that he had some defence against the weather and food to line his belly. He used an old wool poncho to make a shelter. Expertly, he placed a couple of branches, which he'd collected on his journey, against a tree and draped the poncho over to complete the 'house'.

'It ain't perfect but it'll do,' he said.

He hung a pot of snow to melt for coffee and spit a few chunks of meat, from an animal that he'd found, across it. He'd picked up a doe that looked as if it had been mauled by a lion but somehow escaped. Perhaps the lion had found easier prey and hadn't pursued it. The deer's injuries had been too bad for it to survive and he'd finished it off. Stone butchered a few pieces of meat and then left the rest of the carcass to pick up on the way back. It would still be there as he'd roped it and pulled it up a tree to discourage all but the desperate from taking it away. It was a lucky find because the last thing he wanted to do was take time out to hunt and there were few enough animals to track at this time of year.

Dark Star sat with a small squirrel carcass and gnawed at its soft parts before starting to crunch the bones. The horse nosed in the snow to find the grass underneath. Stone looked up at the sky and predicted more snow – it would make the grass for the animal harder to find.

Stone took only a short time out. As soon as he had a

full belly and was rested up, he broke camp, climbed on to the horse and rode off. It took less than a couple of hours to pick up the trail and find Rudyman's cave. Dark Star was an expert tracker and the thick smoke from the mouth of the cave had helped pinpoint it just as surely as if Rudyman had waved a flag to direct him.

Now, Stone sat high in the saddle. His face set in a determined manner as he neared his goal. He anchored his horse's reins firmly and instructed Dark Star to wait, not too far from the horse, and made his way towards his target. He attached wide flat-wired plates on to his boots to spread his weight and make it easier to walk in the crumbly snow under his feet. It was impossible to see the nooks and crannies filled with snow that could trip a man up.

He came across Rudyman who sat as if dazed by his fire. There was no smell of coffee or food and judging by his blue lips, the fool had eaten snow without melting it.

Stone chuckled inwardly. He knew it was time to confront Jon Rudyman. Although he'll find it difficult to answer me with a black frost-bitten tongue, he thought.

'I could play around with his brain a little longer,' he muttered, 'but I don't want him to lose it completely.'

He stepped into the circle of firelight at the mouth of the cave. The flames flickered across his dark expression. Rudyman stared at the 'apparition'. His face was contorted with disbelief and fear. He didn't say anything, just stared as Stone greeted him.

'Hello, Rudyman. I believe you're surprised to see me.'

He picked up the rifle but Stone was quicker. He fired and the firearm spun from Rudyman's hands.

'And that's my weapon you stole, I believe.' He kicked it aside, away from Rudyman. Then Stone picked up his old longrifle. 'Nice to have you back, my beauty,' he said.

He hitched it over his back into his pack but still kept his gaze and scattergun on Rudyman.

'You're dead. I left you near Deadman's Plate.'

'The beast didn't fancy eating me,' Stone said. 'Otherwise I am dead and you're talking to a ghost.'

The comment failed to bring a smile to the other man's lips. Had it managed, Rudyman's lips would've cracked and split with the cold that had already attacked his face. He looked away from Stone and muttered incomprehensibly. Stone caught an odd word about the squaw and a manic sound followed it.

Anything Stone perceived to be about Izusa made him angry. He prodded Rudyman's shoulder with his gun barrel. Unfortunately, for Rudyman, he fell sideways into the fire and the ice on his face sizzled as it melted and burnt the skin away and exposed raw flesh. Stone kicked Rudyman so that he rolled off the embers. He didn't want him to die, yet. Rudyman's eyes had rolled back in his head so the whites were showing. Stone prodded him with the barrel.

'Wake up,' he shouted.

The eyelids fluttered and then opened. Although he'd been frozen and then burnt, Rudyman seemed not to lose the air of insolence as he pulled his body back into a half-sitting position.

'I'll tell you all about that squaw of yours. I want you to know exactly what she was like with me.'

It gave Stone another reason, if one were needed, to hit him again. The butt of the gun smashed into the side of his head and toppled Rudyman over. Stone knelt down by his side.

'I dare you to tell me all about your visit to my cabin.'

Rudyman stared at Stone.

'She's beautiful,' he whispered. 'She looked at me with

those big wide doe eyes as if she was in heaven.' Rudyman screwed up his face into an ugly mush as if mustering all the energy he possessed and spat at Mayle Stone. 'She told me it was the first time she'd had such a man. Her husband was a berdache and liked men best.'

Stone bunched his fist and drew his fingers tight inside his leather gloves. His arm came back and then he let go like a shot from a gun. It had a similar effect. He heard crunch of bone and cartilage and felt Rudyman's face disintegrate under the blows. Then Stone pulled back. He didn't want to leave Rudyman without a face, because he wanted to keep him alive as long as possible. Rudyman rolled over to shield his body from further attack and curled up into a ball.

'Not so brave now, eh?' Stone said.

He watched Rudyman push his face against the snow in an attempt to take the pain away before Stone grabbed at his shoulder and spun him round.

'You're gonna kill me?'

It didn't sound much of a question to Stone, more of a confirmation of the facts.

'Yes,' Stone said. 'But, I promise you, it ain't gonna be an easy death.'

Stone started to kick at Rudyman's lower back. He knew a man would start pissing blood if the boot went in too hard in that particular place. Soon Rudyman coughed blood and lay still. The red patches spreading both at the head and lower body of the man made Stone pause. His anger subsided and was spent momentarily.

He sat on the same small rock he'd found Rudyman perched in front of the fire. The fire, no more than spirals of smoke, caught his concentration and he sat and stared. The smoke danced above the charcoal sticks like a woman dancing. He blinked hard as if to force the thoughts away.

He recalled how Izusa danced around the fire each new moon as if to invite the changes of her womanhood into her, swaying gracefully to an inner music. He smashed the heel of his boot down and scattered the black wood into the snow. Izusa had only known him as a 'gentle' man.

Stone knew he ought not end up a debased human like Jon Rudyman.

He kicked him again.

CHAPTER SEVENTEEN

Mayle Stone sat down by what was once a fire.

He contemplated his future, and of course, Rudyman's future.

Rudyman was alive. He could see his chest moving slowly up and down. Stone's anger still formed a knot inside his chest that for a while at least had taken the place of his heart. He had never considered himself a hard man. He had never felt hate towards another human being and the sight of Jon Rudyman's injuries, which he'd inflicted, sickened him. However, Stone lived by a code of honour. 'An eye for an eye and a tooth for a tooth.'

The law of retaliation, in this new, raw, lawless country of America, seemed sensible to Stone. He banked a few twigs and rekindled the embers to draw the fire. Then as he sat, staring at the flames, a plan formed in his mind.

He decided on a way of making Jon Rudyman confront his own evil deeds. Stone walked back to his horse and then got a rope to put around one of the mules. Dark Star waited but he had a vexed manner about him.

'I know you want to avenge our mistress.' The wolf wagged his tail and his tongue lolled at the side of his mouth as he panted. 'Go.' He pointed towards Rudyman. Dark Star jumped up. 'No kill. Watch.'

His tail dipped slightly but he knew the order. Sometimes Stone used the wolf to guard over his catch and used 'No kill' as a command when he didn't want the catch to be ripped to shreds, merely guarded.

Stone retrieved the deer he'd found and stowed it away. It was easier to get the animal down from the tree than it had been to move it up there. He jumped back to avoid being flattened as the animal crashed to the ground.

'You'd make a hell of a buckskin vest,' he said, 'but I've decided on a better use for you.'

His horse lowered its head slightly and waved its neck from side to side. It acted skittish as Stone pulled the kill along. As the horse's nostrils flared and quivered, he stopped and went over to stroke it and calm it down.

'Easy, now. Ain't nothing to worry about.'

He tied the carcass on to the mule, the proverbial beast of burden, who made no fuss about Stone's activities.

It was an hour later that they returned to the camp.

Everything was as he'd left it. Jon Rudyman hadn't moved. Even without the threat of a wolf waiting to rip him apart, should the thought even enter his head to escape, he was in no state to fight. Stone could see him breathing as his chest moved raggedly up and down. Red bubbles of blood and snot escaped from his smashed nose and blood tinged saliva ran down the corner of his mouth. He nudged the man with the toe of his boot to make sure he was awake and it was met with a sort of grumble mixed with a cry of pain.

'Whatcha want?' Rudyman grimaced. His left cheek-bone had caved in and revealed an upper row of rotten teeth. He used his elbow to prop up his heavy frame. 'Ain't you had your fun?'

112

'You left my woman for dead,' he said.

'She wasn't dead. As far as I know. And she's a squaw! You can pick one of those up for a dime a dozen,' Rudyman scoffed. ' 'Tain't an honest white woman.'

Mayle Stone stared at the piece of so-called humanity and considered the man had an incapacity for feelings. He controlled his temper. Although the desire to kill the man never left him, he wanted the man to feel contrition, sorrow, regret – anything – for his crime.

'Well, I'm gonna be kind to you now. You tol' me you wanted to look into a pair of doe eyes forever?'

Rudyman's face, or what was left of it, looked puzzled. 'That's right.' He started to laugh but he held his stomach as if to hold his guts in. 'You've broken my blame ribs and God knows what else,' he complained.

'I could happily break every bone in your body,' Stone said. He knelt down and whispered, 'Then I'd want to crush every one of those into powder.'

Rudyman frowned. 'OK, so I tarried with your woman and you beat me up. Don't we call it quits here? What happened to that talk of kindness?'

Mayle Stone said nothing. He got up and walked over to the mule. Then he cut down the doe from its back and let the carcass slip to the ground. Rudyman watched. He spat out a wad of mucus.

'What you doing?' he asked.

Stone looked at Rudyman, a thoughtful look on his face, and then answered. 'I'm granting you a wish.'

Rudyman went quiet. The picture reflected in his eyes as he watched Stone slitting the belly of the deer and exposing the entrails, was that of a madman.

Stone snorted and turned his head away from the mess before him. Normally, thick steaming entrails slide out red and viscose after a kill but the animal had been dead for a while and its insides were green and gave off the stink of an angry skunk.

To clean a hide after removing it from the animal, Stone would've stretched it out on the ground, and start to painstakingly scrape it clean. He'd learned this method as a boy and had started to hone those skills when he skinned the grizzly bear he killed many years ago. He did none of this – the animal hide with its stinking flesh was splayed open and left.

'Now get up.'

Jon Rudyman, in a daze about what was going to happen, did as Stone instructed and attempted to stand up. He pushed to get his torso into a sitting position but couldn't manage anything else. Stone put both hands under Rudyman's armpits and helped him to his feet. Rudyman mounted his old broken-winded mule only with Stone's help. Stone leant Rudyman against the mule and then cupped his hands to enable the man to step up. Stone half pushed and half hauled Rudyman on to the back of the mule. The animal was stoic and didn't move.

'Sorry about this, Joe,' Stone patted the mule's neck, 'but I'm sure you're enjoying his suffering.'

The man was weak from loss of blood. He didn't struggle as his hands were tied with rope behind his back and his legs secured under the animal. When Stone started to haul the deer in his direction, Rudyman found his tongue again and started to protest.

'What are you going to do?' he asked.

Stone didn't pause as he answered, 'Tol' you before, I promised I'd grant you the wish of looking into a pair of doe eyes. Only you'll do it until the day you die. I hope you carry the look of them into the hereafter.'

Jon Rudyman started to scream as the dead animal was wrapped around him in a macabre hug. No matter how hard he tried to move his head, its big doe eyes stared at him.

Then Mayle Stone slapped the rump of the now nervous mule and watched as it ran off with its burden into the snow covered valley of Devil's Gulch. He waited until man and mule were so far away he couldn't hear the screams.

That took a wearisome amount of time.

Dark Star, Stone knew, would've happily run after the mule but he held him back.

'Our job is done,' he said. 'We've got to get back to the cabin before we're snowed up here in this valley with Rudyman.'

CHAPTER EIGHTEEN

Ray Heston's suspicion that Mayle Stone had lied to him about Rudyman's whereabouts grew as he made his way towards Deadman's Plate.

Stone was probably after Rudyman, especially after he'd mentioned the reward. Mentally, Heston kicked his own butt. What man wouldn't want to get their hands on $10,000? That amount of money could buy a lot of things. Yet as Heston rode on, he recalled the large amounts of money he'd earned for turning in law-breakers – alive or dead – and wondered what had happened to all the money.

Jon Rudyman was the exception to the rule when it came to earning big money. Heston reckoned on fifty to a couple of hundred dollars with each man he chalked up, maybe the odd one or two netted over a thousand but nevertheless he'd got through it all and with little to show for it.

His horse was good stock. He'd traded in his old horse, with a decent sum of money, for a thoroughbred quarter horse recently. He covered a lot of ground and couldn't afford to rely on a horse over ten years old. He chuckled as he thought of his own advancing age – how many more winters could he cope with as he neared forty years?

'Best put myself out to pasture after this one,' he said. 'This time I'll spend the money well – get a little homestead and a couple of cows.' The horse's ears, which were laid back as if listening to him, twitched. 'Yes, I know it is time to retire when the only person I've got for company is a horse!'

He returned to observing the trail. He could make out that a horse, a mule and a wolf had passed through from the occasional hoof prints, dung and wolf scat that littered the path. That they had come this way, he couldn't dispute, but at what time and what had happened afterwards? That was the puzzle.

Were they old or hard to track as the snow flurries attempted to hide the signs?

Heston recollected that Stone had looked like he'd had a fight with a buffalo and yet the man had shrugged his injuries off and refused to discuss anything. Heston regretted his haste. He'd not returned Stone to the soldiers at the fort because he'd been focused on capturing Rudyman. He'd let Stone go on his way and continued to track the other man. He could've, should've, asked more questions, and then returned him to the fort. If the answers proved false, he'd still have Mayle Stone in custody to interrogate again.

'No point in fretting,' he informed his horse. 'Best put the negative thoughts aside.'

He continued on and saw a suitable resting place. Perhaps one Rudyman and Stone had used so he decided this was as good a place as any to make camp.

'Never miss a chance to rest your horse,' he rubbed his back, 'and never miss a chance to rest yourself.'

He dismounted, took the saddle off and then tethered his horse with a fair amount of rope. Then he made camp.

He collected a few large branches and placed the longest one across two trees and secured it with rope and placed the other branch to make a T shape structure. It only took a couple more minutes to drape a thick poncho style blanket over, and tie the neck end to the T junction and the two sides he secured into the icy ground with sticks. He lit a fire and concentrated on making something warm and filling.

'Can't say this is luxury,' he said, as he pulled a can of beans from his saddle-bag, 'but it's as near as it gets in this wilderness.'

Once coffee and a can of beans were heating, Heston looked around the place. The horse had found a decent patch of grass to graze on and he made sure water was available. He threw a blanket over its back.

'Nights are a bit chilly this time o' year,' he commented as he petted his horse. 'Got one to wrap around me as well, yes, siree.'

Then his glance fell upon a dark brown spot on some grass sheltered from the snow and he knelt down to look at it. His fingers touched on the ground and came away sticky, and when he tasted the substance it was unpleasantly metallic.

'Blood,' he said.

He looked about him as the words sounded uncomfortably loud in the stillness of the hideaway. He drank the coffee after spooning the tin of beans down. All the time his brain was racing – had a murder taken place here? Yet he'd seen Stone so it could only have been the other man, Jon Rudyman. Although, Stone was looking for him so it seemed unlikely.

He poured the rest of the coffee, drank it down then banked up the fire for the night. Heston had to rest before he went after Rudyman. The varmint, or his head, was worth a lot of money and he wouldn't stop until he'd found him.

When he woke up the next morning, his thinking had changed.

'Perhaps I ought to go back and confront Mayle Stone? I believe that man has more answers than I got questions,' he said.

As Stone returned to the log cabin, he chewed over what he ought to do next. He didn't think there'd be any repercussion for his treatment of Jon Rudyman. He imagined that most folks would say he deserved everything he got. His main thoughts were about what was next for him. He had managed well enough for the past eight or so years in Colorado. He didn't want to leave.

'Nowhere to go,' he mused.

Eventually the notions in his head straightened and he supposed he'd stay at the log cabin, because there was no sense leaving just because Izusa wasn't there. He knew it would leave a big gap. And although he never professed to be a religious man, he thought he'd like to stay near her spirit. If he found her bones in the spring thaw, he'd bury her near the little cabin – somewhere he'd walk past every day.

He would also tell Sharka, her half-brother and the rest of the Cherokees, what he'd done to avenge their daughter and sister, Izusa.

That could wait until spring, he thought.

He stopped a couple of times to shoot game with his longrifle and loaded it up on to the mule. The catch was pathetic. Small mammals seemed in short supply and larger animals had the sense to hibernate or stay off the horizon. Dark Star went hunting for victuals but kept near to his master.

The snow came almost horizontally as the wind stiffened into a squall and each snowdrop fastened on every individual whisker on Mayle Stone's face froze. He protected his nose, mouth and ears by tying a scarf around his face. He was thankful for the beaver skin hat on his head. Winter was early.

Through the day and night, he journeyed. He hadn't noticed how far he'd travelled in his pursuit of Jon Rudyman. He pulled over occasionally to let his horse and the mule rest briefly and sat with his slicker wrapped around him for warmth before he continued on. He fought against exhaustion that threatened to overtake him.

Finally, he saw the log cabin and with this in sight, it put a spring into the animals' steps and even under the frost that covered his face, his lips pulled into a smile. He noticed a spiral from the chimney and imagined Izusa returned to the cabin. In his mind's eye, he saw her adding extra fuel to the fire. Then he frowned.

'That can't be true.'

His brow felt hot despite the cold and continued towards the cabin. Then he saw Izusa.

She was waiting at the door to greet him.

Mayle Stone tried to climb out of his saddle but without Izusa's help, he would have fallen off his horse. He felt her strong grip guide him to the bed, take off his wet clothes and then cover him over before spooning hot broth into his mouth.

'Thanks, Izusa,' he murmured, before sleep overtook him.

Occasionally he woke from his uneasy sleep and called her name. He spoke of the time Izusa had revealed her affliction to him.

'I don't care if you can't speak. It doesn't matter about

your tongue.'

He cried out in his dreams at how she'd blushed and closed her mouth, lowered her head in shame.

'Don't run away, Izusa.'

He'd reached out and held her close. She hadn't resisted. He'd held back because he wanted her to feel something for him and not just play the part of the slave she'd been in her tribe.

As he drifted off again, Izusa stroked his brow and spoke soothingly to him. 'Go to sleep,' she whispered.

'Sorry, friend. I hope you'll forgive me for not being your woman when you regain consciousness. All you gonna see is a grisly old man.' Ray Heston drew the covers over the man's naked form and left him to sleep. 'I hope you wake a saner man,' he said.

CHAPTER NINETEEN

When he opened his eyes, Izusa had gone.

Instead he stared at the face of a man he barely knew.

'Don't you recall me? I'm Ray Heston, the bounty hunter.' He didn't wait for an answer as he walked across to the stove and got a steaming bowl of gruel for Stone.

'What have you done with her?' Stone asked.

'Don't know what you're talking about,' Heston answered. 'I got here twenty-four hours before you did. Had time to make a fire and reheat some stew.' He pointed towards the pot. 'Since you arrived a couple a days ago, I've been playing nursemaid. Now eat this.'

Stone pulled his body into a sitting position by using his elbow as a prop and rested his upper back against the headboard. He winced with pain.

'You look as if you've had a bad time,' Heston observed.

Stone growled. He couldn't do anything else at the moment other than take the bowl from Heston. He frowned as he looked around whilst supping from the bowl.

'My woman. That's who I'm talking about,' he said, answering Heston's earlier question. 'I left her here. I think.' He paused and swallowed as if regaining composure. 'She was as good as dead. Jon Rudyman attacked her.

I went looking, couldn't find him and then returned – I was convinced I'd need to bury her.'

'Ah, so that's why you didn't want me around,' Heston remarked. 'You went to avenge your woman.'

Stone ignored him. His eyes held a wild look. 'I can't understand what's happened.'

Heston took the now empty bowl and backed away. He looked puzzled as if he wondered whether he'd get any sense from a crazy man. Then suddenly Stone jumped out of bed, as if the aches and pains that would've knocked back a weaker man didn't exist, and tried to grab hold of Heston by his shoulders.

'Take it easy,' Heston warned.

'Tell me what you've done with her!'

Heston clenched his hands and brought his fists up to Stone's stomach. The effect was dramatic. The little food he'd managed to eat came up again. Stone aired his paunch and then he flopped back to the bed. He passed out.

The peaceful time ended for Mayle Stone when the smile faded from his face and his dreams drifted away the moment he opened his eyes. Ray Heston sat, his legs crossed, on a chair facing him. His shotgun rested on his knee with the barrel pointing towards him.

'Not taking any chances,' he stated. 'Last time you near killed me.'

Stone rolled his tongue across his teeth and lips and grimaced. 'Think you might be overstating things. I feel like the inside of an overfull spittoon.'

'Well, I can't say I've ever been inside a spittoon, but yeah, you look bad.' Heston reached in his inside pocket and fished out a small flat flask. 'You get a taste of this – it'll make you feel better.'

Stone accepted and lifted the flask to his lips. 'Wow! What you got in there? Tastes akin to across between fire and horse piss.'

Heston's face registered offence. 'That's the finest whiskey this side of the Irish sea.'

'Someone has bested you,' Stone remarked. The so-called 'bad' taste didn't stop him taking another couple of swigs, however. 'I reckon anything bad inside me has been a kilt off.'

He handed back the flask and wiped his mouth with the back of his hand.

'Got a bit of stewed boar, if that stomach of yours can take it,' Heston offered. 'I recall you puked the last meal up.'

'As I recall, you punched me in the gut,' Stone corrected. 'Although I must admit, I don't remember that much. I thought my woman was here before. Have I imagined everything?'

'Sorry about that punch. I had to,' Heston said. 'It was me or you. Considering you were half-dead, you acted strong as a buffalo. So let's avoid any friction this time. You wash up, get shucked and then we'll talk.' Heston got up, fetched Stone's now dry clothes and threw them on the bed.

'You sound like my ma, a telling me off,' Stone said.

'Well, I won't use a broom to thrash you.' Heston waved the shotgun. 'You agree?'

'OK.'

The sleep and the whiskey had done the trick, together with the boar meat, and Stone said he felt better for it.

'You said you've been hunting?' he asked.

'Yeah, I left the rest of those carcasses outside, under cover, mind. Reckoned they'd keep in the cold.'

'It's got too dang cold for predators to come nosing

round,' Stone said.

He gnawed the last of the bones. He threw them to Dark Star and thanked Heston, who nodded in agreement but said nothing. It seemed he was waiting for more conversation. Eventually Stone filled in the silence that had developed.

'I've had a rough few days,' he admitted. Then he paused, eyebrows raised as Dark Star chomped on the bones. 'How you manage to stop my wolf from eating you?'

'That wolf was hungry for sure but it preferred the meat I gave him to gnaw rather than taking a bite outta me. I'm a tough ol' bird. An' I tied him up. . . .'

Stone started. 'What?'

'Freed him real quick, though. He don't seem to like fighting when he's stuffed full of boar meat.'

'Yeah. I can see. You and him are the best of friends,' Stone said.

Dark Star looked up and growled.

Heston kept the shotgun handy on the bench next to him. He laughed. 'Wouldn't say that,' he commented. 'Now you gonna tell me what you been up to?'

Stone was quiet. He looked like the effort of conversation was too much for him. Ray Heston closed his eyes for a moment. He decided he ought to give Stone as much information as he could, and that way, perhaps, he'd get something from him without having to prod and poke every bit out.

'OK. Let me start. If you recall, I tol' you the place was empty when I got here.'

Stone's eyes near popped out of his head and he leaned forward. 'I told you, I left Isuzu here. . . .'

For a moment Heston thought Stone would come across the table. He moved his seat back.

'Easy, easy,' he said. 'It was empty. I knew someone had been here. A bowl of what I took to be stew was half ate and there was an empty flask as well. The bed was stripped but I could see spots of blood like from an injury. I followed them out, down the porch an' then a couple of more spots sunk in the snow.'

Stone's expression collapsed from anger into despair.

'Then what did you find?'

'Nothing. Then I went out hunting and shot the boar and a couple of other things too stupid to hibernate. I warmed the gruel, the stuff I first gave you, while I was preparing the game,' Heston continued. 'If it was your wife, she was long gone.'

'Had a mule been taken?'

'Don't know your situation, friend. There was one mule in the stable before you brought in your horse an' another mule. And a cow. I tried to milk her but she's near to drying up.'

Mayle Stone's gaze darkened with despair. 'I left Izusa here, with food, water and her wolf to guard her. To keep her safe.' Stone stared at Heston. 'What about the wolf? Where is it?'

Heston's eyebrows lifted with a frown. 'Ain't no wolf hereabouts except that one.' He pointed at Dark Star. Then he shuddered. 'An' one wolf brings a pack around.' His hand went to his shotgun as if to make sure while his glance took in the locked windows and door. 'Now I tol' you all I can, friend, how about you come clean about Jon Rudyman? I tol' you that varmint has a $10,000 reward on him. A man could do a lot with that. Where is he?'

'I'm not interested in Jon Rudyman now. All I want to do is find Izusa.'

Heston shook his head. 'No. You help me find the outlaw an' I'll help you to find your woman.'

Stone looked at the man's resolute face. He gave the impression of being someone who'd never give up. And he'd given a promise that he'd help find Izusa.

'Last time I saw Rudyman he was heading down the valley, Devil's Gulch, a few miles from Deadman's Plate. He ain't going far. That place can suck you up and what's spit out ain't worth worrying about.'

'We've got some meat that I stored outside to take with us. You'll help me track Rudyman down.'

'I ain't going with you,' Stone protested. 'I've told you where he is. I'm off to find my woman. My wife.'

'That's not the plan. You sent me on a wild goose chase last time. This time we'll go together. Soon as I find him, I'll keep the other half of our agreement.'

'You fail to keep your word,' Stone said as he packed some provisions and found extra ammunition for his lon-grifle, 'an' I'll kill you.'

Heston laughed. Spat in the palm of his hand and held it out toward Stone.

'Deal done.'

CHAPTER TWENTY

The wind howled around the cabin and snow drifted up to the shuttered openings. The snow didn't melt when it trickled its way inside but merely hardened to tiny icicles.

'I think we ought to wait a while before we go out,' Stone said.

Heston disagreed. 'If we wait, winter will set in and we'll both be stuck in this cabin. Not that I don't like your company, friend, but you ain't my idea of solace on a miserable dark night.'

Stone grinned despite his reluctance to set off again. His mind could only concentrate on one thing – what could have had happened to Izusa?

'Not as if Rudyman's gonna go far,' Stone persisted. 'His body will freeze out there.' The thought should've cheered him, yet his face turned sour with worry. 'She will freeze out there.'

The last words were spoken softly as if to himself.

'Anyone out there will likely perish,' Heston said. 'So we'd best be off. And I don't want hungry vermin eating his body. Got to have some evidence to claim my reward . . . our reward. I said I'd share some of it when we first met.'

'Everyone is bent on sharing their ill gotten gains,'

Stone replied. 'Money don't mean the same out here in the wilderness.'

Heston stared. 'That might be so for you but it means something to me. I've stored a whole pile of dreams on that reward money.'

The mules were loaded up again and the men dressed in slickers hunched over their horses and faced the biting wind.

Dark Star followed Stone faithfully.

'That wolf is more of a hound than any hound I've ever known,' Heston commented. 'I could do with finding myself a hound like that.'

Stone nodded. 'Takes a lot of rearing and patience. I found it as a cub. I killed their ma.'

After that, conversation was limited. It was too cold and both said they reckoned their tongues would freeze if they tried to wag them with small talk.

The snow skimmed the ground, not settling any place yet as the wind blew it into drifts. The animals held their heads low and they plodded stoically along. The route was straight, as any place in the mountains, and they kept a good pace. They broke their journey only when exhaustion threatened them all. They melted snow for the horses, cooked a hot meal and brewed strong coffee.

On the evening of the second day, they came to the place were Stone had loosed Rudyman into the valley.

'We'll soon find him,' Stone reckoned.

Heston said he wanted to continue through the night, but common sense overrode the notion.

'We'll take a couple of hours sleep when it gets dark then start over as soon as dawn breaks.'

Stone nodded.

This agreed, they rode on until stars decorated the night sky.

Heston looked up. 'Do you imagine there are any other places like this up there?'

'What?'

'I mean, any other worlds with men, like us, trekking all over the place?'

Stone looked up, screwed up his eyes to get a better view. 'Well, Heavens up there somewhere,' he observed. 'The good book tells us that Hell's underneath us. I judge that's enough for the Almighty to worry about.'

'I suppose,' Heston agreed.

'Anyways, let's get on with here and now.' Stone pointed to some rocks with one that overhung to provide shelter. Heston tied the horses and mules while Stone made a fire and heated up beans and meat stew and coffee.

'Don't think we need to keep watch. A good fire will keep wild animals away.'

'You're right. In my view, most two legged beasts will keep to their own hearth. Except us two madmen,' he added.

They both used their saddles as pillows and they tried to settle down to sleep. However, their first attempt only lasted about an hour. The sound stirred Stone first. He sat up and shook the sprinkling of snow that had found its way underneath the primitive shelter they'd constructed. It was the sound, not the cold, which made him shiver. At first, he wondered if it was a pack of coyotes that sang out in the night. A yowling noise came intermittently against a constant background that Heston, who was now also awake, described graphically, 'It's the sound of hoofs on hard ground. The iron shoes are scratching over rocks. It hurts my damn teeth an' I ain't got that many.'

They now both stood, longrifle and shotgun in hand, back to back, and listened.

'You heard this before?' Heston asked.

'No, and if I never hear it again it will be too soon,' Stone replied.

'Probably only the wind,' Heston said.

'Yeah, right,' Stone agreed.

Neither sounded confident about those conclusions. The decision was made to stay where they were and investigate, as planned, in the morning.

They made themselves comfortable again but both slept, with one eye open.

At first light, bereft of real rest, they got up and consumed a hasty breakfast. The sky was lit up red as the sun rose through the inversion layers of cloud. Only the daylight and the beauty it brought with it didn't quite erase the horror of those gruesome sounds and they set off again, their haunted expressions clear for anyone to see.

'I'm sure it was all a bad dream,' Heston commented.

Stone dispelled the idea. 'You keep saying that if it helps,' he said. 'However, I don't usually share my dreams with anyone.'

'Likely it was wolves killing prey.'

Stone's face showed disbelief at that suggestion but he couldn't offer another explanation.

Perhaps, they decided, it was better to agree with something that held a string of logic rather than dwell on an unnatural reason.

There were no tracks to follow. Whoever, or whatever, had disturbed them had gone. Neither commented about the sounds again but the general consensus seemed to be one of relief.

The next night brought more of the same. They didn't try to sleep this time. For a while they sat back to back, watched, but saw nothing.

Then Heston said, 'We gotta find out what this is about. Sure shakes the insides out of me.'

Stone agreed. 'My belly feels queasy as well.'

They saddled up and followed the sounds. It was a difficult task because the horses' ears lay flat and the animals trembled. They coaxed them on until the horses started to rear up on front legs. The mules' reaction was to stop still and pull against their lead ropes.

'We ain't gonna get far on these frightened beasts,' Heston moaned. 'Let's tie them up securely. I'll hobble them, because we can't afford to lose them, and we'll walk up there – it's just a couple of hundred yards. We might see something over the rim of that hill.'

Stone agreed, but said, 'I'm turning back then. There's no sign of Rudyman and this was the route I sent him, tied to the back of his mule. I don't want to corner something meaner than me.'

Heston stared at Stone. He shivered as if someone had walked over his grave. 'Tied to the back of a mule? What the dang did you do that for?'

Stone sometimes thought that silence is the best answer. As he looked at Heston, whose eyes glittered black in the darkness, he decided this wasn't the right choice now. He calmly explained what had happened.

'I had no choice. He'd destroyed my life – that is, my life with Izusa. I paid him back.'

Heston paled. He said nothing but stepped back from the man.

'I suppose I might have done the same,' he admitted, however, he kept his distance nonetheless.

They had little time for any more conversation, because the noise reverberated around them again. In the darkness, it was hard to see what was happening. However, they made out the shape of a man coming towards them – a faceless man on a mule.

'Who are you?' Heston called out. 'Stop or I'll fire.'

The rider didn't stop and Heston fired his shotgun as the thing was almost on top of him. The bullets met nothing but air and mule and rider continued onwards. The two men threw themselves out of its way and fell on the ground. Stone rolled over. He fired into the man's back. The bullets seemed to have no effect. Soon the rider turned, and sideways they saw a madman staring into the face of a doe, and then it was on them again.

'Run!'

The cry came from both Stone and Heston.

The pair split and let the rider through as a scream worse than a sound from Hell came from the apparition.

Both men ran to their mounts, un-hobbled them and they were riding off in moments. Fortunately, the pack mules were still tethered to the saddles, and all sped away from the frightening 'thing' that screeched and tried to reach out to them.

The 'thing' didn't give up easily and now it pursued the two men.

Heston barely kept his head covered. The neckerchief he wore flew off and his leather hat bobbed up and down, barely tied on with a string fashioned from plaited gut. Stone still had on his beaver hat, secured with strips of leather. The wind blew their slickers out like tents and allowed the snow to drench their clothes and melt into their boots. As they fled for their lives, neither seemed to give too much thought to those things and continued to ride as if the devil was on their backs. They goaded their mounts to move faster and adrenaline kept them warm for now.

Every so often, both Stone and Heston turned to fire but although on target, it gave them no respite. The bullets were wasted, as it seemed the shots went through the apparition. Right up to the edge of the valley, they were chased. As they rode out of Devil's Gulch, a howl echoed around the walls of the canyon. Their foe turned and rode around the valley, yet again.

'Well, what was that?' Heston asked.

'Not quite sure,' Stone replied. And yet his expression told Heston he was sure.

Heston looked at Stone.

'I believe you know that was Jon Rudyman's ghost haunting Devil's Gulch.'

'Yeah. I told the poor broken-winded beast to keep riding and that's what has happened.'

'That's rotten to do that to an animal,' Heston admonished.

Stone disagreed. 'I don't go with that,' he said. 'Rudyman always treated the beast badly. The mule hadn't been allowed to rest in life, and now, it won't let Rudyman rest in death. As I saw the mule ride off, I could've sworn there was something like a grin on its face.'

'Sounds a damn silly idea to me.'

Stone nodded. 'Maybe, can't say for sure. Now I've led you to Rudyman, I'm going home.'

'Well, I'm for going onwards. I ain't letting nothing keep me away from my reward. You promised to come with me.'

Stone raised his eyebrows. 'I took you this far. That's as far as I go. You go and find your treasure and I'll go after mine.'

Heston laughed. 'Never thought of him as a treasure afore,' he mused.

Stone watched Heston pull up his collar and fasten the top button of his coat. 'I hope you don't encounter that thing again,' he said.

'Just a trick of light,' Heston said. 'That thing can't be no ghost.'

It seemed to him that the day had chased the horror away.

'Best of luck finding out the truth of that,' Stone answered.

'Of course, you won't get any reward,' Heston warned. 'Once I got him, I'll be carrying up the trail to the nearest large town. Although I did promise you I'd help you find your woman.'

Stone nodded. 'I'll look for Izusa. Thanks for the offer.'

'Goodbye and good luck,' Heston said. He turned his horse, briefly touched his hat to Stone and was off in pursuit of Rudyman.

'You too,' Stone answered.

CHAPTER
TWENTY-ONE

'Good judgment comes from experience, and a lotta that homes from bad judgment.'

Heston sat on his horse and considered the wise words he'd heard a while ago. He couldn't recall the author but the words held strong. There'd been many times in his life he'd made some piss-poor judgements but he'd gained both good experience and valuable wisdom from the outcome of those judgements. At this moment, he was about to go into Devil's Gulch where an ogre, ghost, spirit or a madman was riding around, out of control.

'Now is that a good or bad decision?' he murmured. He thought about his life now. He spoke to his horse again. 'I'm a bounty hunter. Nothing wrong with that but it's a young man's game. I could stop. . . .' He paused as he stroked his horse's mane. 'The thing is I ain't got no money. This'll net me enough to retire.' The horse's ears flicked back and forth rapidly. 'I know,' Heston continued, 'ain't a horse's life, either. Although if we get through this together then you're gonna have a stable like you can't imagine and enough green grass and grain to keep your belly full forever.'

Heston pushed his shotgun into the saddle holster. 'I like you, my beauty, but I think a plain old Dragoon – my wrist breaker – is gonna be my best friend to fight this devil.'

Heston had won the sabre in a poker game from an old timer who'd fought in the Mexican war.

'I fancy you'll do the job for me,' he said.

Mayle Stone also pondered on whether he'd made the right decision to leave Heston.

After the encounter with the 'mad mule man' they'd stayed in camp until daylight. When Ray Heston had finally made the decision to go after Rudyman, Stone had shrugged his shoulders and started the journey back to the log cabin. However, the nearer he got to home, the more he considered his options. The cabin would be cold, empty and be filled with so many memories of Izusa, he'd feel the need to cry like a baby and end up being thought of as crazy as a loon.

Eventually he'd also have to face the Cherokees and let them know what had happened. It was possible they'd want to avenge her death and take it out on the nearby white settlers, too. Although not responsible, they had the same attitude as white folk and to them, one settler looked exactly like another.

In the end, Stone returned home, stabled the mules, rested the horse, milked the cow and again considered the idea of going back to help Heston.

He felt obliged to help the man with his task of getting his reward money. The other consideration was that he wanted to avoid the inevitable – the return to a solitary life.

Heston decided he'd be in for a drawn-out wait and made a sturdy camp. It took all day. By the time night came, he was exhausted but protected from the elements and warm. He'd quickly found a spot between two trees and tied a log across them. From a couple of short logs, placed on the ground underneath what would become a shelter, he made a bed. He lay four thick branches, stripped clean with an ax, over the logs and used two stakes to stop them rolling. It took the longest time to get the stakes into the ground, which got harder as the day lengthened.

'Ain't nothing fancy but it's sure better than sleeping on the frozen ground.' His horse looked up but made no comment and then continued to graze.

It took him several hours to lay branches against the log he'd tied to the tree and then to thatch it with extra bits of wood and leaves.

The red sun threatened to dip beneath the horizon far too early for him to complete all his tasks. However, before that happened, he'd managed to clear a patch for the fire and make it on stones that would retain the heat over the next couple of days.

He had to watch for his prey because he knew that this was no ordinary man. Indeed, from what he'd seen, he suspected that he was dealing with the devil on horseback – albeit in the guise of a ghostly spectre and a mule.

Although the mule and man appeared only at night, Heston decided he ought to use the daytime to track. He could use the light to search out the places Rudyman could hide. There had to be a place where they holed up together until nightfall. Frightened as he and Stone had been a couple of nights ago, he had no truck with ghosts and tales of horror.

They're for folks with overactive imaginations.

He left the camp and turned east where few trails seemed to exist and he had to bushwhack through the meandering valley, taking care not to lead his horse where unknown dangers might lie. Part of him enjoyed the absolute solitude of the place but part of him feared what he might find in the wilderness.

It was on his second venture out that he came across the sight, which he feared would stay with him until the end of his days.

Heston dismounted, to give his horse a rest and though he didn't admit to being saddle sore, he was glad to stretch his legs for a while.

There is a harsh beauty to winter, he thought. He looked at the sun hung over the mountains, weak and yellow – almost like a child's spinning toy.

Today, the wind was at half-strength and allowed him to look out over Devil's Gulch without losing his hat. He could see the snow up there and assayed that the tops were never free of ice. He could see where sheets of ice floated over a lake.

'I bet soon even the fish will freeze,' he said. 'That's somewhere I'll definitely avoid at night.'

There were no trails for him to follow. Either the snow packed hard into ice and horses' hoofs left no marks, or the wind caught the falling snow and blew it into drifts. He noticed indents in the rock walls of Devil's Gulch, although more similar to caves than cracks.

'Guess I'd best mosey up and take a look.' His hand went to his sabre to reassure him it was there. 'Don't want to be on the menu for some hungry lion or wolf.'

The third indent in the wall proved deeper than Heston expected.

'Dang, that could hide a lot of trouble.' He went back to his horse and took out a couple of pine pitch sticks to light his way along. He moved slowly and carefully. 'Don't want to startle anything,' he whispered. His own voice comforted him and took the edge off the fact he was totally alone.

The flare lit up the cave walls. Then suddenly he was in a chamber. He had the sense of being in the bowels of Hell.

'I can see why this valley is named Devil's Gulch.'

The hairs on the back of his neck stood on end, made him feel cold, and he shivered. He carefully made his way into the depths – he wanted to see the whole place and check it out. Rudyman could be hiding in a place like this, he thought.

Then he saw it.

His hand tightened on the spluttering pine resin stick. He tried to swallow but his throat felt tight.

'Dang and blast,' he cried. The stick fell from his hand as he tripped over a rock on the floor. His other pine sticks followed. He was in a velvet blackness that ate up the light. It was so dark it felt solid. Immediately he was on his hands and knees and scurried around like a beetle.

'Where did they go?'

In the darkness, he felt things crawl and swish under his hands – things that felt as if they should never exist. They crawled up his sleeves and vest and tugged at his chest and then got into his boots and sucked his toes. Heston took deep rapid breaths. He could feel and hear everything. His other senses were magnified now he was unable to see.

'Stop it!' he admonished. He braided at his own cowardice. 'What are you? A Molly?'

He recalled the saying that 'there was nothing wrong with being afraid, it's what you do with that fear' and that fact helped as gradually he calmed and ignored the sensations of monsters in the dark.

'Got you!'

He picked up the pine resin stick and then pulled a small knife and stone from his pocket. He held the stick between his knees and worked to make a spark.

The place was light again.

Heston lit a couple more resin sticks and then wedged them between small rocks.

'If I fall over again, I won't look like a mush-head. I'll be prepared.'

His sense of well-being and his self-congratulatory mood disappeared in an instant.

'What in tarnation?'

There, a mere six feet away, was a man sitting on a mule.

CHAPTER TWENTY-TWO

Away from the dwelling, Sharka pondered what to do. Izusa could not stay. A daughter did not return to her family home. Then she decided as soon as Izusa had regained her strength, she'd send her son back to Grizzly Bear with Izusa.

Her daughter would return to him.

She turned to go back to the village but the old medicine woman intercepted her.

'I wanted to speak to you,' Noname said.

'We have been together all day while you helped me tend to my daughter,' Sharka countered.

'We have indeed and I could see how you swaddled her as if she were a baby.'

'I did not.' Sharka frowned. 'I was concerned about her health.'

'Had you been that concerned you would have called me earlier.'

'When the wolf arrived at the village, it was decided that you would accompany my son in his mission to find Izusa.'

'Yes, it was Wolfie who didn't reject my help.'

She used a nickname for him. She was Noname the

medicine woman. She had her own set of rules and no one corrected her. 'I am talking about why you didn't bring her to me when she was a baby. You constantly rejected my help.'

'Izusa was so strange with those big white eyes. Then white hair. Big Heart said she was a monster.' She looked down at the ground as if there was something to find. 'I told her she was a monster.'

Noname ignored Sharka's tears. 'Big Heart, bah!'

Sharka looked up. No one should ever speak the name of the Cherokee tribal chief with such disdain.

'He did his best. He was generous.'

'I don't think so.' The old woman dismissed Sharka's profession of loyalty. 'He ignored her, you mean. Then she was cast out. Who else's daughter has been offered to a pale face?'

'There was a council meeting before it was agreed. It was taken into account that the man Grizzly Bear saved me, and Izusa. It was as if she'd been chosen for him.'

'It was written in the stars?'

Sharka chose to overlook the sarcasm in the old woman's words. 'Yes. That is so.'

'Why did she flee from him?'

Sharka's eyes clouded with tears. 'We will never know the truth,' she said. 'You know she will never be able to tell us.'

'That is your fault. Your fault, Sharka, that Izusa has led such an awful life.'

The old medicine woman seemed to puff out to twice her size. The bulbous eyes seemed ready to explode and her mouth opened and shut as if words were impossible to form. At last Noname calmed down, breathing deeply and whispering prayers to her ancestors.

Sharka had felt the full force of Noname's anger. It

wasn't a physical beating but her words had the same effect and she shielded her body as if warding off blows. The younger woman didn't move. She sought to control her trembling body as she clasped her arms around herself. Finally it was quiet again.

Noname paused but only to regain her breath. 'And now you understand why it was so important for you to bring the baby to me?' Sharka just stared. Her face held no expression. 'I could have set her tongue free.'

Sharka found her voice at last. She defended her role as a mother. 'I protected her. No one else loved her. I don't believe it's possible for you to help. She can't move her tongue properly. You cannot change it. No one can help.'

'I can put her in a deep sleep and do it.'

'No. No! I won't let you.'

'I will ask her. It is her choice. She is a woman.'

Big Heart agreed that for the time being Izusa should remain with Noname, the medicine woman. He listened to Sharka's objections but managed to persuade her to leave the future to fate.

'Izusa has returned here. I don't know why. It is more than two days' journey to Grizzly Bear's home even without the blizzards to mar the way. We will find out why she left him or whether he sent her away, sometime, but not now.'

Sharka knew the argument made sense. They had no idea what had happened. They didn't know if he was alive. It would be pointless to send Izusa back to an empty home.

'Yes, everything must wait,' she agreed.

Izusa gradually improved with Noname's care. Her affliction, her tongue-tied mouth, had been cured with the aid of a sharp knife and many herbal remedies and magic chanting.

Noname taught Izusa to speak.

After many lessons to pronounce her words, Izusa was forced to speak. The words were garbled and Izusa shed many tears in the effort to make Noname understand what she said. One of Noname's tricks was that Izusa would not be offered food, or drink, or warmth if she didn't ask. It worked.

A change came within the village when a child accidently swallowed a shiny stone. Its mother screamed for help as she tried to gouge the stone from its throat. Izusa heard the cries and ran to the group that had gathered round. Everyone rushed away from Izusa and her white wolf except the mother and her child. Immediately Izusa pulled the child, whose face was turning blue, to her. Its mother began to protest but then stood and watched as Izusa put her hands under the child's ribs and pushed in and upwards until the shiny stone coughed out and the child took a gasp of air.

Izusa handed the child to its mother. 'Your son will be well now. Just keep it away from shiny stones!'

Izusa settled into a routine and the old medicine woman said she enjoyed the hours she spent teaching Izusa all the names, qualities and uses of the plants they gathered. Izusa had a natural gift as well as a background of helping Sharka with this chore.

There was Partridgeberry to be collected. Noname used it to speed up and ease the pain of childbirth. Dogbane, prepared as a tea for contraception, was given to any woman who asked for it. She discovered that Yellow root, boiled into tea, helped stomach pains and a Feverwort concoction would help to cure fevers. She collected Green

Hellebore to relieve body aches and pains. She learned to chew Trumpet Honeysuckle, ready to apply to bee stings.

'I'll never remember all these names,' Isuzu said. 'Or the uses of the medicines.' She tucked a strand of white hair behind her ear and pulled the brimmed hat down to protect her eyes from the sun.

'You will,' Noname assured her. 'You have learned so much in such a short time.'

'Noname,' Izusa asked, 'why is it that my people do not treat me like a monster now?'

'You were never a monster, Izusa,' Noname answered. 'Different, yes. And since you saved that boy they have seen how you have been gifted with the power of healing.'

With the start of autumn, when the majority of flowering herbs were collected and hung to dry, came the question that Noname had expected for some time.

'Is it time to return to my Grizzly Bear?'

'You don't say 'return home'?' Noname queried.

Izusa looked down. Something she hadn't done for a while.

'I don't know where home is,' she answered.

'You need to find out,' Noname said.

CHAPTER TWENTY-THREE

Mayle Stone came across Ray Heston's camp easily. It wasn't hard to find, he knew where they'd parted and where he was headed. So he had to be somewhere between there and the next place in Stone's reckoning. He added logs to the smouldering fire. It burst into life and blazed out warmth. He was practised in taking care of himself in the wilderness.

Heston, however, was nowhere to be found. Stone thought of trailing after him but the camp looked as if Heston had every intention of returning to the place. Stone decided to rest up and wait on the following day.

A couple of roasting rabbits spit over the fire, a wolf happily chewing part of the catch and Mayle Stone felt at peace with the world.

Rey Heston stood and stared at the discovery of Jon Rudyman and the mule. Both seemed to have been petrified by the water that dripped from the roof above them.

'Impossible,' Heston whispered. His voice sounded

loud in a place so silent even the sole of his boots boomed as he placed his feet on the ground. 'A man can't fossilize.'

Curiosity got the better of his trepidation and he moved towards them. It was then he noted that the pair had been frozen solid.

'Makes more sense, I suppose.'

These explanations made the tightness across his shoulders and back disappear and his rigid stance became more relaxed and he sighed and breathed slowly. He was still tense but now he believed he had the courage to do what he'd come here to do.

He sawed through the frozen shackles of rope that bound Jon Rudyman to the mule with his small knife. Heston felt the cold through his gloves and stopped occasionally to shake his hands and get the blood flow back to his fingertips. He would've have liked to use his sabre but the height of Rudyman was at the wrong angle. He knew he had to get the man off the mule first before he could chop off his head.

When Rudyman hit the ground, it seemed as if a piece of glass had shattered into a million shards around his feet. It was merely an allusion and it was only ice crystals that were scattered over the ground. The mule crumpled in a manner that suggested it was glad to be rid of the burden.

Heston wasted no more time. The speed of his actions underlined the fact he wanted to move swiftly and leave the underground cave.

'It's not natural,' he muttered. 'Nothing is real in here.'

He took his sabre and chopped Rudyman's head clean from his body. There was no blood – the heart hadn't pumped anything round his body for a long time.

'Don't believe you ever had a heart,' Heston said.

He grabbed at the straggly hair on Rudyman's head and

held it up, ready to drop it into the leather sack he used for these occasions.

There'd been too many, he thought.

He still joked when he did it – helped take the edge off a macabre chore.

'My god, Rudyman, you're not a pretty sight.'

Heston looked at the beard, almost as long as the tangled locks, and watched the insects that had infested it drop out. Heston shuddered and stamped on them, in case they wanted a new host but the things were already dead and cracked and split underfoot. Rudyman's gnarled ugly face with its staring eyes, one green and the other brown stared out from the wrinkled sun-leathered skin.

'I bet you've always been able to back a buzzard off a gut wagon – which is where your mother probably threw you after she gave birth!'

Heston tied the bag with a leather thong and turned to start the journey back to camp. He glimpsed the mule from the corner of his eye and stopped.

The animal looked tearful. Its head rested on its front legs. Common sense and experience told Heston his imagination was working too hard.

'I'm getting plumb weak north of my ears,' he grumbled. Yet his endeavour to talk sense into himself failed. He put the bag down and went back to the mule. 'Can't leave you here like this. I think you've earned a bit of respect after all that ill treatment you've suffered. Can't bury you, Joe,' Heston apologized, to the dead mule. 'I'll cover you with rocks.'

Heston looked at the finished job. The pile wasn't high. The mule had been small but the effect was that the animal was less diminished by death than it had been by life.

*

'Just about to come and look for you.'

Heston took in the comfortable camp where Mayle Stone lay on the bed he, Heston, had made and tucked up in front of a blazing fire.

'Yes, I can see that.'

Stone got up and went to the couple of pots strung across the fire. He poured a cup of coffee and handed it to Heston.

'You look like a man who's been catawamptiously chawed up,' he commented.

'Well, I sure ain't been on a bender,' Heston replied.

'I'll dish up some stew. Make you as hearty as a buck.'

Mayle Stone didn't ask Heston anything. The man gulped down the coffee; the rabbit and bean stew went down quick enough to choke before he grunted he needed sleep. Stone didn't mention, as Heston crawled on to his bed and pulled his hat over his face as if to blot out the world, that his hair had turned snow white.

Stone made do with a few branches he'd pushed together and covered with a waterproof for his bed. He took a while, twisting and turning to get half-comfortable. Heston's snores, which came after thirty seconds of touching his head to his saddle pillow, were that of an extremely tired man.

Both men woke to a sound that made their follicles contract and the hair rise all over their bodies. Stone looked at his hand as if he expected bumps the size of goose eggs to be there. Heston sat up and his mouth pulled back towards his ears as he tried to scream, 'Wh ... wh ... what. . . ?'

'It's the same sound we heard all those nights ago,

before I left you,' Stone answered. The terror on his face reflected in Heston's wide-eyed stare.

'No, no, that ain't possible.' Heston scrambled towards the leather sack he'd placed at the foot of his bed. He fumbled with the leather thong before he grabbed at his knife and split the top open. 'Look here.' He held aloft the head of Jon Rudyman.

Startled, Stone looked at it. Revulsion was written all over his face. He puked. He held his stomach and aired his paunch like a silly chickabiddy who'd taken his first taste of deadshot.

Both men were on their feet. They'd slept in their trousers, shirts and boots and now pulled on jackets as they clutched at their guns.

'Don't think these are much use,' Heston muttered. 'I cut off the fellow's head and buried the mule.' He looked over at Stone. 'I was being respectful like.'

Stone didn't laugh. He agreed with Heston. 'It needed that,' he admitted, ''cause that beast never had any repute before.'

They had no more time for veneration because before they could think of any more compliments for the animal, the outlaw and the mule galloped through the camp. Sparks of fire jumped on to the clothes and blankets and fire spread over the saddles.

The horses and the pack mules screamed and squealed. The horses reared up and yanked at the rope. The mules were hobbled but it didn't stop them putting as much distance as possible between them and the apparition.

Stone and Heston fired at the departing spectres and tried simultaneously to beat out the fire. Neither had any effect. They watched as their accouterments flared up and turned black.

'We've got to get out of here. This truly is Devil's Gulch

now. Don't fancy being bushwhacked again.'

'No. You look a bit grey haired now,' Heston laughed. The sound was more hysterical than jolly.

He stared as if contemplating the comment. Then said, 'Yeah. We both got a few now.'

Both men stood and surveyed the camp. 'Ain't much left.'

'I get the feeling we're being warned off.'

Heston held the leather bag up and studied it. The head had melted into an unrecognizable mass. 'Well, there goes my ten thousand doolars. I had plans for that money. I was gonna buy myself a nice little homestead and settle down and . . .'

He stopped as he noticed Stone scrutinizing him.

'You sure you'd be happy with those things? Perhaps you've had too many years just wandering and being alone . . . it'd be hard to settle down.'

'That go for you, youngster? You were happy alone, you tol' me, until that little Injun . . . I mean, Izusa . . . turned up at your door. Turned your thoughts to wedlock.'

Stone scuffed snow across the smouldering embers of the campfire. 'That ain't gonna happen. I'm back on my ownsome now.'

'You don't sound bothered by it,' Heston commented.

'Everything is a bag of nails at the moment. I can't think straight.'

'You could come out West and go prospecting with me. If I hadn't got tangled with Rudyman, I meant to go to California. I've heard that the streets are paved with gold.'

'No, thanks. My pa looked for gold. Got into so much debt he blew his brains right out his head. I'll go back to my cabin. Stay a while. Think things out.'

Heston nodded. 'I understand. I've finished head-hunting.' He laughed and held up the sack.

152

Stone grinned. 'Let's rack and scrape our stuff – what's left of it.'

As the sun started to glance above the mountains, both men had waved goodbye and gone in opposite directions.

CHAPTER TWENTY-FOUR

The snow came early and very deep that winter.

December saw a freak thaw that turned snow to water.

Mayle Stone stayed indoors. He had plenty of food and the animals were dry and fed with hay stored in the stable. It turned out to be fortunate as the cold weather moved back and formed a crust of ice, which made foraging food for animals impossible.

A trek to the fort for emergency supplies was unthinkable as a blizzard followed the cold front and snow built up to six feet and snowdrifts, Stone guessed, were twenty feet in places.

It wasn't until late March that the weather eased.

The horse, mules and the cow ran around like they'd been let out of gaol. Stone felt stir crazy too and pleased to breathe fresh air and walk on the ground where a couple of green shoots were breaking through. He hunted and got a deer for him and Dark Star to feast on. He hacked out the innards and threw them on the ground for the wolf, then butchered the rest into pieces small enough to stew or roast over the fire. He hung most of it high in the cabin roof to be dried out by the smoke from the fire.

He took up life as he'd left it before the incident in Devil's Gulch. The only thing he missed was Izusa's company. He often walked in the early summer to the cabin he'd built but then it became too painful because the wood had started to disintegrate and succumb to the harsh weather of the Rockies. He'd learned that Colorado weather could change drastically over a day as well as throughout the year. Cold winters plus boiling sun in summer wore down both man and nature bit by bit.

Yet he'd hoped to find her bones. To bury. Out of respect of their friendship rather than sentiment. However, he found no trace of her.

He spent all summer stocking up for winter. He visited Fort St Vrain. Nothing changed except for a new commander. Second Lieutenant Peterson had been promoted and returned East. Storekeeper Wilkins still tried to short-change everyone but was tolerated because there was nowhere else to buy the produce he stocked. There was plenty of talk about a 'ghostly spectre' terrorizing any travellers stupid enough to go near Devil's Gulch.

'Not that I believe in that nonsense,' Wilkins said. He filled the flour bag right up to the top under Mayle Stone's watchful eye. Then he came close enough for Stone to catch the man's bad breath. 'Some folks say it's the ghost of Jon Rudyman.'

Stone drew away from the mixed smell of sulphur and stale food. 'Folks will say anything. Why, if you let the story go around, you'll have a stampede of people at your door. All wanting coffee and needing supplies.'

Wilkins's eyebrows met in the middle in a frown and then he smiled as if the thought had never occurred to him before.

'You could be right,' he agreed.

*

Autumn was the season to take stock.

As Mayle Stone walked around stables filled with grass to get the livestock through the next winter, he slapped the cow on the rump. She mooed loudly and swished her tail at the outrage. Stone laughed.

'Seems the bull came a courting and you didn't chase him away.'

He'd arranged with a smallholder, about four hours' ride away, to put the bull to the cow and promised if the result proved successful he'd give him a choice of furs as payment.

It would take another six months before a calf appeared in springtime but by that time, new forage would be growing to nourish both cow and calf.

There was salted and smoked meat and flour, oats, beans, salt – he wasn't a fancy cook but he'd stocked up on the basics – and whilst the cabin wasn't stacked to the rafters with ammunition, common sense inclined him to be wary and make sure he had plenty of everything.

'Me and you, Star, we'll do some hunting any day the weather is clear.' The wolf stood at such a height that he could place his paws on Stone's shoulders – as he was now inclined to do – and licked at his face. 'Whoa, boy, don't you try and eat me!'

The wolf was both his companion and bodyguard. Dark Star always walked at his heels now and wherever he went, nobody spoke out of turn to a man who was part Cherokee Indian and had a wolf as a champion.

He stroked the fur of Dark Star's coat. It would soon thicken to acclimatize to anything the winter could throw at him. It made Stone recall the bearskin he'd taken from the grizzly. Where was it now? The recollection brought an avalanche of memories to the fore. He found the bear's claws and whiled away the hours polishing and threading them on to a leather thong.

He tied it around his neck and touched it for luck.

'I wish I knew what had happened,' he said to Dark Star.

The wolf suddenly yapped, barked and then howled. It sounded eerie to Stone's ears.

'You know something I don't?' He stepped outside and looked around. Something had disturbed the wolf.

Stone put his hand to his eyes as a visor. He made out a couple of dots on the horizon. One was a merely a blur as it preceded the other.

Dark Star acted in an excited manner. He began yapping again and then howls which lasted for a second and then increased to ten seconds in length filled the air.

'What is it?' Stone asked again.

The answer came with an answering howl that cascaded across the distance between them. A note with a single tonal quality, which flexed from low to high, and then back again to low.

'Moon!' Stone cried. He went to follow Dark Star who had decided to greet the now grown pup of his birth pack. Then he held back.

Silently he watched the two wolves stand shoulder to shoulder; fur bristled, tails wagging and ears erect as they sniffed each other's noses and muzzles in greeting.

Stone's gaze fixed on something that looked more like an apparition.

Izusa had returned.

He ran towards her. He picked her up and spun her around. She grinned and held on to his neck. Then he placed her on her feet again.

'I thought you were dead. I looked for your bones – to bury near your cabin.'

'I had to leave. I believed that man had spoilt me.'

'That man,' anger crossed Mayle Stone's face, 'that man will never hurt you again.' Then puzzlement replaced the anger. 'He didn't hurt you?'

'Not in one way,' Izusa said. 'It was why I left because I, I mean, I thought I'd been defiled. It was merely my first moon time.' She lowered her head. 'For some reason I was later than other women.'

Mayle Stone's breath came in a loud gasp. 'I'm so happy you weren't harmed. Whatever, Jon Rudyman will never cause anyone grief again. He'll have to square it with his maker, though.'

She offered him the bearskin she held in her hands.

'I took it because I was cold. Now I return it and say thank you.'

Stone spluttered as he took the skin as if something had suddenly dawned on him. He looked in askance. 'What? I mean, Izusa – you can talk.'

The pale cheeks blushed. 'The medicine woman healed me. I was tongue-tied.'

'Your hair and skin – it's white.'

Izusa frowned and tucked the loose hair behind her ears. 'I don't want to offend you. I realize my ugliness has always made me an outcast.'

'No,' Stone added, hastily, 'you're beautiful. You were lovely before but you always hid yourself under the mud.' Then he confessed. 'I saw you once – fresh from the lake.' The look on his face changed from happiness to sadness. 'When you reappeared, later in the cabin, your hair, your skin, it was dark again.'

Izusa laughed. Dark Star stopped his greeting to Moon and now his ears lay flat. With his lowered tail tucked between his back legs, he looked ready for fight or flight. He seemed undecided. Stone reassured the animal.

'Yes, it is an unusual sound, Dark Star.' He held his hand out towards Izusa. 'I hope we will hear it frequently.'

Dark Star went towards Izusa. His muzzle relaxed and he sniffed at the hand she'd held out towards him.

'And will you stay?'

Stone had invited Izusa into the cabin. They'd both eaten and now shared a honey sweetened drink made from the roots of the Sassafras tree prepared by Izusa.

'It has many medical properties to keep the body healthy,' she explained.

'Tastes good, too,' Stone agreed.

She looked across and smiled and the firelight lit up her eyes and they appeared like pink opals.

'You haven't answered my question.' Stone reminded her about his invite as he gathered up the dishes. Her eyelids started to close but he stepped across the room and held her closely. 'That is your way of avoiding things,' he said. 'You shut your eyes and hope no one can see you.'

'I'm sorry,' she answered. 'Something I learned many years ago.'

'You'll stay, tonight at least?'

'Yes. I'll stay. I belong to you. I am in exchange for the wolfskin.'

Stone lowered his arms. His desire to kiss her didn't seem as strong when she offered herself in such a manner. He knew it to be true. She was given to him.

'I don't hold you to that,' he said. 'I took you in because I didn't think you'd be allowed back into the Cherokee village. Has that changed?'

Izusa explained. 'Noname the old medicine woman took me under her wing. She cured the affliction of my tongue. She taught me how to take her place. She is old. Very old.' It was as if Izusa now considered what she'd said.

159

'No. I don't mean I have to stay with the Cherokees.'

'You must do whatever is best for you,' Stone said.

Izusa stayed and slept in the pallet bed.

Each day she looked out towards the horizon as if waiting for someone.

Stone told her to go.

'Go back home, Izusa.' He pressed a finger to her lips. 'It isn't here. It's with the Cherokees. Take up your calling as a medicine woman. You've collected so many herbs this month there won't be room for my food.'

She laughed and then laid out the tiny packets she'd fashioned. 'This will help you if you get any fevers, this will mend cuts or sores and this—'

'You've already explained,' Stone interrupted.

She laughed again. He winced at the pain Izusa's laughter brought. It was like the tinkle of tiny bells. He would miss her.

Then she became serious again.

'Can I keep Moon?' Moon sat at her feet. His head tilted to the right, his eyes quizzical and his tongue lolled out as he panted. They both waited for the answer.

'He's always been your animal,' Stone said. 'Take care of her, Moon.'

Moon howled in answer.

Stone escorted Izusa to the Cherokees. He went only as far as the outskirt of the village.

He lifted Izusa from the mule.

'If you want to,' he said, 'you can always return.' He took the bear's teeth from his neck and handed them to Izusa. 'Don't forget me.'

He watched as she ran, turned to wave and then she disappeared with Moon at her heels.

160